STORIES BEYOND
TIME AND SPACE

THE **G**LOBE **R**EADER'S **C**OLLECTION

STORIES BEYOND TIME AND SPACE

ROBERT R. POTTER

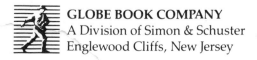
GLOBE BOOK COMPANY
A Division of Simon & Schuster
Englewood Cliffs, New Jersey

ROBERT R. POTTER received his B.S. from the Columbia University School of General Studies and his M.A. and Ed.D. from Teachers College, Columbia University.

Dr. Potter has been a teacher of English in the New York City School System, a research associate for Project English at Hunter College, and a teacher of English at the Litchfield (Conn.) High School. He has held a professorship at the State University of New York and now teaches at the University of Connecticut's Torrington branch.

Dr. Potter is author of Globe's *Tales of Mystery and the Unknown, Myths and Folktales Around the World, English Everywhere, Making Sense, Writing Sense, Writing a Research Paper, Language Workshop* and the consulting editor of *American Folklore and Legends* and the *Pathways to the World of English* series.

Edited by David J. Sharp
Illustrations by Charles Molina

Cover Art: *The Persistence of Memory*, Salvador Dali Collection, The Museum of Modern Art, New York.
Cover Design: Marek Antoniak

ISBN: 0-83590-158-0

Printed in the United States of America.
10   9   8   7   6   5   4   3

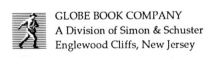
GLOBE BOOK COMPANY
A Division of Simon & Schuster
Englewood Cliffs, New Jersey

Contents

Plunging In

Prolog
John P. McKnight 1

Appointment at Noon
Eric Frank Russell 9

The Fun They Had
Isaac Asimov 17

Mr. Lupescu
Anthony Boucher 25

Test
Theodore L. Thomas 35

The Oval Portrait
Edgar Allan Poe 45

The Perfect Woman
Robert Sheckley 53

Rolling Ahead

The Mathematicians
Arthur Feldman 63

Mrs. Hinck
Miriam Allen de Ford 71

The Flatwoods Monster
  Frank Edwards 85

The Mansion of Forgetfulness
  Don Mark Lemon 93

Who's Cribbing?
  Jack Lewis 101

In Our Block
  R. A. Lafferty 113

The Room
  Ray Russell 125

So You Too Can Write Sci-Fi?
  K. Ripke, L. Leigh, T. Bruey 133

Reaching Outward

Examination Day
  Henry Slesar 145

The King of the Beasts
  Philip José Farmer 155

Something Green
  Fredric Brown 161

The Gift
  Ray Bradbury 177

The One Who Waits
  Ray Bradbury 185

Finis
  Frank Lillie Pollock 199

The Wonder of Science Fiction

Did you ever wonder?

Not wonder *about* something. Just wonder?

Of course you did. Life would be dull if you didn't wonder about things. For thousands of years people have wondered about things. They wonder at the stars in the sky. They wonder at the miracle of human birth. What makes human beings grow and stop growing? What makes them laugh and weep and love? They wonder what life might be like on other planets. How would things seem to creatures from another world? What will the end of the world be like? People would not be people if they didn't wonder. That's the wonder of wonder, and that's what science fiction is all about.

A scientist does experiments in his laboratory. A science fiction writer does experiments in his mind. He asks himself "What if . . ." and "Why . . ." and "Just suppose. . . ." In this book you'll meet many such problems: *What if the government decided that all people really* must *be equal? What if creatures from outer space one day landed on Earth? Why did people first invent words and start talking to each other? Just suppose you had to crash-land a small space ship on the far-away planet of a distant sun?*

A few of the stories that follow could happen in your community tomorrow. Most of the tales, however, will take you far out in time or in space. In "The Fun They Had," you'll go to school in the middle of the twenty-second century. You'll also meet "The Perfect Woman" of the year 3000. In "The Room," you'll live in a future world completely filled with advertising. You'll meet "The One Who Waits" on Mars, and you'll find that the distant planet called Kruger III might be a very comfortable place, if only there were "Something Green."

Science fiction is written for people who think. You will find the reading questions after each story a real help in understanding it. You'll also find that thinking critically about important subjects in a new way can be a lot of fun.

Why sci-fi? Because life is wonder-full.

Prolog

John P. McKnight

*Let's start with a switch. Many science-fiction
stories happen in the future. Let's begin by going
back into the past—way, way back to the dark
days when people lived in caves and ate what they
could find in the forests.*

Prolog (or prologue*) is a word meaning
"introduction" or "beginning." When you finish
the story, you'll see why it's the best possible
prologue this book could have. For it's also a
prologue to every book that was ever written, and
to every story that was ever told.*

Sound impossible? Read on.

Vocabulary Preview

AIMLESSLY (AIM less lee) without aim or
definite purpose
  • Julie spent study-hall period drawing
  aimlessly in her notebook.

DROWSE (DROWZ) to fall half asleep
  • Carl woke up at seven, but *drowsed* in
  bed till after eight.

GRUB (GRUB) a small worm-like creature
  • Eric jumped when he saw the *grub* on
  the leaf in his hand.

GRUNT (GRUNT) to make a deep throaty
sound
  • People talk, birds sing, and pigs *grunt.*

LEDGE (LEJ) a narrow flat place
  • The mountain climbers stopped on a
  ledge to rest.

PERIL (PER ul) danger
  • The mountain climbers took every step
  in constant *peril.*

SABER-TOOTHED (SAY ber TOOTHT) having
teeth like a saber, or sword
  • The *saber-toothed* tiger no longer
  exists.

SHARP SOUND CRACKED IN THE QUIET OF the morning, and the hairy man-creature drowsing before his cave came suddenly awake.

In one quick movement, he was on his feet. He turned to the young one, where it lay on the deerskin at the mouth of the cave. But the child slept peacefully, no danger near it.

Awkwardly, the man moved then to the edge of the narrow stone ledge. Blinking against the spring sunlight, he looked out across the tall trees to the river below. There at dawn and at dusk the animals came to drink. But now, its bank was quiet.

In the valley a small tree bent. A moment after, the crack of its breaking reached the man. A great, dark shape appeared for a moment in the shade. The biggest beast was feeding.

Without thinking, the man reached for the sharp stone he had found at the river bank two winters ago. He held it in his hand; his fingers fitted closely against it. It was a good thing, this stone. With it, he had cut up the deer the evening before, and killed the creeping thing curled up before the cave this morning. In some ways, it was a better thing than a club. If he had a club, with a stone like this at its end . . .

The man looked about him once more, and went back to his place near the child. He squatted there; and almost at once his eyes closed again.

The man drowsed in the sun because he had fed to his full the night before, and there was still meat in the cave. Coming back empty-handed from the hunt, he had found the deer, recently killed but only half-eaten by a saber-toothed tiger.

He had carried the torn body of the deer up to the cave, and the woman had held the sweet tender meat over the fire they kept always burning. They had eaten until their swollen stomachs would hold no more.

Awaking in the bright dawn, the man was still full. A cold bone and some grubs he found under stones near the brook were enough to eat now. So he sat sleeping in the sunshine, motionless except for his fingers that explored the mat of hair covering his chest and belly. Now and then the searching fingers found some lice; and these the man, grunting in sleepy victory, cracked between powerful jaws and ate. The bites were tasty, and satisfaction at getting rid of an old enemy provided the sauce.

Beside him now, the young one woke. It moved on the deerskin, waving its hands and kicking its feet. It made little wet grunting sounds. Across the man's mind, as he listened sleepily to the child's syllables, there flowed pictures of the brook that bubbled down the hillside. "Wa, wa, wa," went the child; the man thought of the clear cool water splashing over the big rock where he sometimes sat to watch the slender fish in the green depths of the pool below. "Coo, coo," the child piped; the man thought of the birds in the tall trees calling to each other at dusk.

But then, the child's noises changed. They grew unhappy. Its lips, moving loosely against toothless gums, made the sound, "Ma, ma." Over and over, it cried, "Ma, ma; ma, ma."

Disturbed, the man started to rise. But the woman was there before him, quick and silent on bare feet, taking the child up from the skin, holding it to her. At once, the child's cries stopped; there was the soft slup-slup of its lips.

In the man's brain, memory stirred. Dimly, he remembered another child—the child that the great saber-tooth had carried off before their eyes. That child, too, had cried at times, and made the sound "ma, ma" when it was hungry.

4

And at the sound, he remembered, the woman, leaving her jobs in the cave, had gone to it.

The man took up the sharp stone again and began scratching aimlessly at the rock of the ledge. Something about the pictures in his brain excited and disturbed him. They awakened in him the same hidden worry he had known the day he climbed all alone to the top of the highest hill and gazed out across the endless flat ground beyond the river. He got to his feet, tossing black hair back from his sloping forehead, and went to the edge of the ledge to stare down toward the river. But its bank was quiet; the valley too was empty; in the forest, nothing moved.

Behind him, the woman put the child down and, noiselessly, went back into the cave. The child cooed, and grunted, and was at last silent. The man turned to look at it. It was sleeping again.

In the growing warmth, the man's mind wandered. On a time many winters past, memory told him, he himself had been a child. And so he must once have been a tiny helpless creature like this one, that cried when it was hungry and fed only when the woman came. He wondered if he had made the same noises that this baby, and the other, made when they were hungry. Silently, he shaped his thick lips to form the sounds. . . .

A leaf rustled behind him. He turned, in sudden awareness of danger.

In the low bushes beside the cave mouth, a great wild dog crouched. It was thin from hunger. Its red-rimmed eyes were fixed on the sleeping child.

Silently, belly to ground, the dog crept toward the tiny child. In the instant after the man turned to see, it was near enough. It crouched for the leap forward.

The man's eyes measured quickly. He was too far away.

He could not reach the child in time.

Before he could cover half the distance, the dog would

jump, fasten its dripping jaws on the baby, and be off into the woods.

A moment the man stood frozen, in the shock of helplessness.

Then his lips shaped to remembered sounds. To his surprise the great roar of his voice filled the stillness.

"Ma, ma!" he yelled. "Ma, ma!"

The dog turned. It flashed its teeth at the man. Then its eyes went back to the child; it crouched again.

But as it did, the woman appeared in the cave mouth. Old practice of peril helped her. In an instant, she had picked up the child and stepped back to safety.

The dog's spring fell on the empty deerskin, and at the man's rush it ran off into the woods.

Carrying the child, the woman came back.

The man's brain at last reached the end of the thing that had disturbed it.

He put out one hand and pointed it at the woman.

"Mama," he said. "Mama."

He had learned to talk.

Recall

1. In the beginning of the story, the man drowses and does little because (a) in his day, women did all the work (b) his stomach is full (c) it's probably a weekend.

2. The man values the stone because it (a) is the kind of rock used as money (b) is beautiful to look at (c) has many possible uses.

3. The child's noises suggest to the man (a) pictures of things he's seen and heard (b) real words the child will someday speak (c) the nights that the baby has kept him awake.

4. After being fed, the child (a) plays with the man (b) toddles to the edge of the ledge (c) goes back to sleep.
5. Which statement is accurate? (a) Called by the woman, the man saves the baby. (b) Called by the baby, the woman gets there on time. (c) Called by the man, the woman saves the baby.

Infer

6. Just as the wild dog comes, the man is about to (a) eat breakfast (b) say "Ma, ma" (c) get up and go hunting.
7. The story is one author's idea of the invention of (a) thought (b) language (c) cooking with fire.
8. The people in the story probably looked (a) just like us (b) a little like us (c) nothing like us.
9. The characters in the story can most reasonably be called (a) robots (b) beasts (c) cavepeople.
10. The story contains little conversation (talking) because (a) the noise would probably attract wild animals (b) it would have been in a foreign language (c) the characters can't talk.

Vocabulary Review

1. A *saber-toothed* tiger could accurately be called a (a) grub (b) peril (c) ledge.
2. The word *saber* means (a) loud (b) ugly (c) sword.
3. The *grub* crawled *aimlessly*. In other words, (a) the ant crawled upward (b) the hog crawled upward (c) the worm crawled this direction and that.
4. The best place for a person to *drowse* is on a (a) waterfall (b) mountain cliff (c) lawn chair.
5. A *grunt* is sometimes indicated by the word (a) "Whee!" (b) "Ugh!" (c) "Click!"

7

Critical Thinking

1. The introduction to this story stated that it was "a prologue to every book that was ever written, and to every story that was ever told." Explain in your own words why this is true.

2. Why is it important to the story that the child's noises suggested certain things to the man? Why is it important that the man wondered about his own noises as a child? Why is it important that the child's sound when hungry was "Ma, ma"?

3. "Prolog" is a skillfully written story. Many things in the first part point directly at the exciting ending. The reader who misses these things gets less out of the ending. For instance, the first paragraph is nearly repeated when the dog arrives. What else in the first part of the story can you connect with the ending?

4. Look back at the third paragraph from the end. What question has the man been asking himself? What is the "thing" that has been disturbing his mind?

Appointment at Noon

Eric Frank Russell

The story that follows is about a man you won't forget. His name is Henry Curran. At first he seems a strange character for a science fiction tale. He lives in the here and now. He's ALL BUSINESS. He's always on the go, a tiger of a man, big, rich, and powerful. He pushes buttons and people jump. He shouts and people shake. One day Henry Curran meets a character from "beyond time and space." When that happens, he learns an ageless lesson—and you will too.

This is an important story. Don't read it simply to kill time. You'll soon see why. . . .

Vocabulary Preview

APOLOGETIC (uh POL uh JET ik) filled with apology; admitting fault
• Ramon said he was sorry, but he really didn't seem to be very *apologetic.*

APPOINTMENT (uh POINT ment) an agreement to meet someone
• Heather's *appointment* with the dentist was changed to 2:45 P.M. Friday.

DIMENSIONLESS (dih MEN shun les) without dimensions—width, length, and height.
• The explorers on the mountain were trapped in a *dimensionless* cloud of mist.

DISMISSAL (dis MISS ul) the act of ordering or allowing to leave
• The principal ordered an early *dismissal* because of the snowstorm.

MOUTHPIECE (MOUTH peese) slang for lawyer
• The criminal's *mouthpiece* said his boss was out of the country.

PRECOGNITION (pre kog NISH un) knowledge of something before it happens
• Fortune-tellers claim to have the gift of *precognition.*

SOMBER (SOM bur) very sad; gloomy
• The criminal left the courtroom with a *somber* face.

HENRY CURRAN WAS BIG, BUSY, AND SUCcessful. He had no patience with people who weren't successful. He had the build of a fighter and the soul of a tiger. His time was worth a thousand bucks an hour. He knew of nobody who was worth more.

And crime did not pay? "Bah!" said Henry Curran.

The law of the jungle paid off. Henry Curran had learned that nice people are soft people, and that smiles are made to be slapped.

Entering his large office with the fast, heavy step of a big man in fighting shape, Henry threw his hat onto a hook. He glanced at the wall clock. He noted that it was ten minutes to twelve.

Seating himself in the large chair behind his desk, he kept his eyes on the door. His wait lasted about ten seconds. Frowning at the thought of it, Curran reached over and pushed a red button on his big desk.

"What's wrong with you?" he snapped when Miss Reed came in. "You get worse every day. Old age creeping over you or something?"

She paused. She was tall, neat, and steady. She faced him across the desk. Her eyes showing a touch of fear. Curran hired to work for him only people he knew too much about.

"I'm sorry, Mr. Curran, I was—"

"Never mind the excuse. Be faster—or else! Speed's what I like. SPEED—SEE?"

"Yes, Mr. Curran."

"Has Lolordo phoned in yet?"

"No, Mr. Curran."

"He should be through by now if everything went all right." He looked at the clock again, tapping angrily on his desk. "If he's made a mess of it and the mouthpiece comes

11

on, tell him to forget about Lolordo. He's in no position to talk, anyway. A little time in jail will teach him not to be stupid."

"Yes, Mr. Curran. There's an old—"

"Shut up till I've finished. If Michaelson calls up and says the *Firefly* got through, phone Voss and tell him without delay! And I mean without delay! That's important!" He thought for a moment. Then he finished, "There's that meeting downtown at twelve-twenty. God knows how long it will go on. If they want trouble, they can have it! If anyone asks, you don't know where I am. You don't expect me back before four."

"But, Mr. Curran—"

"You heard what I said. Nobody sees me before four."

"There's a man already here," she got out in an apologetic voice. "He said you have an appointment with him at two minutes to twelve."

"And you fell for a joke like that?" He studied her with a cutting smile.

"I can only repeat what he said. He seemed quite sincere."

"That's a change," snapped Curran. "Sincerity in *my* office? He's got the wrong address. Go tell him to spread himself across the tracks."

"I said you were out and didn't know when you would return. He took a seat and said he'd wait because you would be back at ten to twelve."

Without knowing it, both suddenly stared at the clock. Curran lifted an arm and looked at his wristwatch to check the instrument on the wall.

"That's what the scientific bigbrains would call precognition. I call it a lucky guess. One minute either way would have made him wrong. That guy ought to bet money on the horses." He made a gesture of dismissal. "Push him out—or do I have to get the boys to do it for you?"

12

"That wouldn't be necessary. He is old and blind."

"I don't give a damn if he's armless and legless—that's *his* tough luck. Give him the rush."

Obediently she left. A few moments later she was back. She had the sorrowful look of a person whose job forced her to face Curran's anger.

"I'm terribly sorry, Mr. Curran. He insists that he has a date with you for two minutes to twelve. He is to see you about a personal matter of great importance."

Curran scowled at the wall. The clock said four minutes to twelve. He spoke with purpose.

"I know no blind man and I don't forget appointments. Throw him down the stairs."

She hesitated, standing there wide-eyed. "I'm wondering whether—"

"Out with it!"

"Whether he's been sent to you by someone else, someone who'd rather he couldn't tell who you were by sight."

He thought it over and said, "Could be. You use your brains once in a while. What's his name?"

"He won't say."

"Nor state his business?"

"No."

"H'm! I'll give him two minutes. If he's trying to get money for some church or something he'll go out through the window. Tell him my time is valuable and show him in."

She went away and brought back the visitor. She gave him a chair. The door closed quietly behind her. The clock said three minutes before the hour.

Curran sat back and looked at his guest, finding him tall, thin, and white-haired. The old man's clothes were black, a deep, somber black. They set off the bright, blue, unseeing eyes staring from his colorless face.

Those strange eyes were the old man's most noticeable feature. They were odd, as if somehow they could look *into*

13

the things they could not look at. And they were sorry—sorry for what they saw.

For the first time in his life, Henry Curran felt a little alarmed. He said, "What can I do for you?"

"Nothing," replied the other. "Nothing at all."

His voice was like an organ. It was low, no more than a whisper, and with its sounding a queer coldness came over the room. He sat there unmoving and staring at whatever a blind man can see. The coldness increased, became bitter. Curran shivered despite himself. He frowned and got a hold on himself.

"Don't take up my time," advised Curran. "State your business or get to hell out."

"People don't take up time. Time takes up people."

"Just what do you mean? Who are you?"

"You know who I am. Every man is a shining sun to himself, until he is dimmed by his dark companion."

"You're not funny," said Curran, freezing.

"I am never funny."

The tiger light blazed in Curran's eyes as he stood up. He placed a thick, firm finger near his desk button.

"Enough of this nonsense! What d'you want?"

Suddenly holding out a lengthless, dimensionless arm, the man whispered sadly, "You!"

And Death took him.

At exactly two minutes to twelve.

Recall

1. Miss Reed has difficulty telling Henry Curran about (a) certain phone calls (b) an important letter (c) the old man waiting to see him.

2. The appointment is not actually "at noon" but at (a) two minutes to twelve (b) two minutes after twelve (c) four o'clock.
3. Curran finally agrees to see his visitor (a) when he first learns he's blind (b) because he believes the old man might have been sent by someone else (c) right after he remembers making the appointment.
4. The most noticeable thing about the old man is his (a) clothing (b) voice (c) eyes.
5. At the end of the story, Death is described as having (a) a white robe (b) a lengthless, dimensionless arm (c) a long beard.

Infer

6. Miss Reed works obediently for Curran because (a) he pays her double salary (b) she is a close relative (c) he knows something about her that she doesn't want known.
7. Curran's discussion of possible phone conversations indicates that he (a) never talks on the phone himself (b) is involved in criminal activities (c) is worried about death.
8. The words *coldness, shivered,* and *freezing* are used toward the end of the story to indicate that (a) the heat of Curran's life is rapidly fading (b) something's wrong with the heat in the building (c) inside, Curran stays cool.
9. The sentence "Time takes up people" means (a) dead people go to heaven (b) as time passes, young people grow taller (c) after a certain period, death comes to everyone.
10. It is reasonable to believe that if Miss Reed had entered Curran's office at noon, she would have discovered that her boss had (a) been shot (b) committed suicide (c) suffered a heart attack.

Vocabulary Review

1. A *somber mouthpiece* is the same thing as a (a) loud trumpet player (b) serious boxer (c) gloomy defense lawyer.
2. A word that combines a prefix meaning "before" with a root meaning "know" is (a) *apologetic* (b) *precognition* (c) *dimensionless.*
3. If you were late for an *appointment,* you would probably be (a) *apologetic* (b) *dimensionless* (c) *somber.*
4. A person cannot possibly be (a) *apologetic* (b) *dimensionless* (c) *somber.*
5. The word *dismissal* usually refers to (a) being late (b) length of stay (c) leaving.

Critical Thinking

1. At what point in your reading did you know who the old man really was? Look back at the last section of the story. What clues help reveal the old man's identity?
2. The meaning of this story can be expressed quite simply in a short sentence. Write that sentence on a separate sheet of paper.
3. Usually an author has four main ways of showing us what a certain character is like. Good readers look for four kinds of clues: (a) direct description or other statement by the author; (b) what the character says; (c) what the character does; and (d) how other characters react to him or her.

Find one sentence in the story that serves as an excellent example of each kind of "character clue." Write these sentences on your paper. Explain in your own words what each lets us know about Henry Curran.

The Fun They Had

Isaac Asimov

No collection of science fiction tales would be complete without a story by Isaac Asimov. A scientist, teacher, and writer, Dr. Asimov has probably done more for sci-fi than any other person now living. In fact, his own life seems like something out of sci-fi. He was born in Russia in 1920. His family moved to the United States when he was a small child. A top student, he decided on a career in chemistry. Writing sci-fi stories to help pay expenses, he worked his way to a Ph.D. (doctor's degree) in 1948. For a while he taught at a university and continued with his sci-fi writing. Finally he left the classroom to write full time. At least "full time"! At last count he'd published 174 books and hundreds of magazine stories. Many of his tales, like "The Fun They Had," are set in the future.

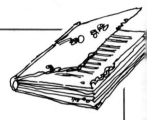

Vocabulary Preview

CALCULATE (KAL kue late) to figure out
  • Ann can *calculate* the speed of a moving car within five miles per hour.

DISPUTE (dis pewte) to argue about
  • Few customers *dispute* what the cash register says.

MECHANICAL (muh KAN i kul) having to do with machines
  • The Ramos family has a new *mechanical* dishwasher.

NONCHALANT (NON shuh LAHNT) casual; cool; completely unworried
  • How can Yvonne appear so *nonchalant* on the stage?

PUNCH CODE (PUNCH KODE) holes punched in a card to form a message
  • Mom's paycheck always has some kind of *punch code* on it.

SCORNFUL (SKORN full) full of disapproval
  • Dad examined my report card with a *scornful* face.

SECTOR (SEK tur) a part or area of something
  • The riot started in the southern *sector* of the city.

M

ARGIE EVEN WROTE ABOUT IT THAT night in her diary. On the page headed May 17, 2155, she wrote, "Today Tommy found a real book!"

It was a very old book. Margie's grandfather once said that when he was a little boy *his* grandfather told him that there was a time when all stories were printed on paper.

They turned the pages, which were yellow and crinkly, and it was awfully funny to read words that stood still instead of moving the way they were supposed to—on a screen, you know. And then, when they turned back to the page before, it had the same words on it that it had had when they read it the first time.

"Gee," said Tommy, "what a waste. When you're through with the book, you just throw it away, I guess. Our television screen must have had a million books on it and it's good for plenty more. I wouldn't throw *it* away."

"Same with mine," said Margie. She was eleven and hadn't seen as many telebooks as Tommy had. He was thirteen.

She said, "Where did you find it?"

"In my house." He pointed without looking, because he was busy reading. "In the attic."

"What's it about?"

"School."

Margie was scornful. "School? What's there to write about school? I hate school." Margie always hated school, but now she hated it more than ever. The mechanical teacher had been giving her test after test in geography and she had been doing worse and worse until her mother had shaken her head sorrowfully and sent for the County Inspector.

19

He was a round little man with a red face and a whole box of tools with dials and wires. He smiled at her and gave her an apple, then took the teacher apart. Margie had hoped he wouldn't know how to put it together again, but he knew how all right and, after an hour or so, there it was again, large and black and ugly with a big screen on which all the lessons were shown and the questions were asked. That wasn't so bad. The part she hated most was the slot where she had to put homework and test papers. She always had to write them out in a punch code they made her learn when she was six years old, and the mechanical teacher calculated the mark in no time.

The inspector had smiled after he was finished and patted her head. He said to her mother, "It's not the little girl's fault, Mrs. Jones. I think the geography sector was geared a little too quick. Those things happen sometimes. I've slowed it up to an average ten-year level. Actually, the over-all pattern of her progress is quite satisfactory." And he patted Margie's head again.

Margie was disappointed. She had been hoping they would take the teacher away altogether. They had once taken Tommy's teacher away for nearly a month because the history sector had blanked out completely.

So she said to Tommy, "Why would anyone write about school?"

Tommy looked at her with very superior eyes. "Because it's not our kind of school, stupid. This is the old kind of school that they had hundreds and hundreds of years ago." He added loftily, pronouncing the word carefully, "*Centuries* ago."

Margie was hurt. "Well, I don't know what kind of school they had all that time ago." She read the book over his shoulder for a while, then said, "Anyway, they had a teacher."

20

"Sure they had a teacher, but it wasn't a *regular* teacher. It was a man."

"A man? How could a man be a teacher?"

"Well, he just told the boys and girls things and gave them homework and asked them questions."

"A man isn't smart enough."

"Sure he is. My father knows as much as my teacher."

"He can't. A man can't know as much as a teacher."

"He knows almost as much I betcha."

Margie wasn't prepared to dispute that. She said, "I wouldn't want a strange man in my house to teach me."

Tommy screamed with laughter, "You don't know much, Margie. The teachers didn't live in the house. They had a special building and all the kids went there."

"And all the kids learned the same thing?"

"Sure, if they were the same age."

"But my mother says a teacher has to be adjusted to fit the mind of each boy and girl it teaches and that each kid has to be taught differently."

"Just the same, they didn't do it that way then. If you don't like it, you don't have to read the book."

"I didn't say I didn't like it," Margie said quickly. She wanted to read about those funny schools.

They weren't even half finished when Margie's mother called, "Margie! School!"

Margie looked up. "Not yet, mamma."

"Now," said Mrs. Jones. "And it's probably time for Tommy, too."

Margie said to Tommy, "Can I read the book some more with you after school?"

"Maybe," he said, nonchalantly. He walked away whistling, the dusty old book tucked beneath his arm.

Margie went into the schoolroom. It was right next to her bedroom, and the mechanical teacher was on and waiting for

21

her. It was always on at the same time every day except Saturday and Sunday, because her mother said little girls learned better if they learned at regular hours.

The screen was lit up, and it said: "Today's arithmetic lesson is on the addition of proper fractions. Please insert yesterday's homework in the proper slot."

Margie did so with a sigh. She was thinking about the old schools they had when her grandfather's grandfather was a little boy. All the kids from the whole neighborhood came laughing and shouting in the schoolyard, sitting together in the schoolroom, going home together at the end of the day. They learned the same things so they could help one another on the homework and talk about it.

And the teachers were people. . . .

The mechanical teacher was flashing on the screen: "When we add the fraction $\frac{1}{2}$ and $\frac{1}{4}$ . . ."

Margie was thinking about how the kids must have loved it in the old days. She was thinking about the fun they had.

Recall

1. The children find reading a real book strange because (a) the language is so different from theirs (b) the printing is old-fashioned (c) the words don't move.
2. The book the children have is about (a) machines (b) schools (c) science.
3. The children in the story learn their lessons (a) in a school building (b) at home (c) while asleep.
4. The job of the "County Inspector" seems to be to (a) quiz children on their lessons (b) make sure proper school hours are kept (c) adjust teaching machines to fit individual children.

5. One advantage of the machines over today's teachers is that (a) the machines can make each lesson fit the individual learner's mind (b) all the machines have a good sense of humor (c) machines cost less.

6. The word "they" in the title refers to (a) students in the year 2155 (b) near-human machines of the future (c) students of today.

Infer

7. Margie is surprised at Tommy's finding a book because (a) Tommy's family can't read (b) real books are almost unknown (c) Tommy is blind.

8. The word *telebook* can't be found in a dictionary. In the story it is used to mean (a) a book about TV (b) a TV set that shows the pages of real books (c) a TV screen that shows moving words.

9. The reason homework has to be done in a punch code in 2155 is probably that (a) children can't write very well (b) paper is scarce (c) machines can't read and respond to ordinary handwriting.

10. The story suggests that students of the future will learn (a) many foreign languages (b) subjects we cannot even imagine today (c) subjects very much like today's subjects.

Vocabulary Review

1. A *sector* of a map would be (a) the border of the map (b) the price of the map (c) an area on the map.

2. A *scornful* person would be most likely to (a) act in a nonchalant manner (b) complain a lot about things (c) know how to calculate rapidly.

23

3. A *nonchalant* person would be most likely to (a) complain (b) work too hard (c) whistle.
4. Cards with *punch codes* on them are (a) used for most gambling games (b) widely used as fool-proof report cards (c) easily sorted by a machine.
5. A student who can *calculate* well is likely to get high marks in (a) a foreign language (b) math (c) hygiene.
6. A student with a *mechanical* mind would be likely to enjoy working after school in a (a) pet store (b) flower shop (c) garage.
7. A person who wants to *dispute* everything is likely to be (a) studious and shy (b) generous with his friends (c) hard to get along with.

Critical Thinking

1. The story lists one advantage of machines over regular teachers. Think of at least three disadvantages.
2. Suppose that the world of 2155 really is like the world in the story. Do you think most students will share Margie's feelings about "school"? Explain.
3. How likely do you think it is that books will have disappeared by 2155? Explain. How likely is it that humans will no longer function as teachers? Explain.
4. If machines *do* replace teachers by 2155, what reasons will have accounted for the change?

Mr. Lupescu

Anthony Boucher

It's hard to know what to call the well-written story that follows. It's fastasy, yes, but it's all too real. It's both a science-fiction tale and a murder mystery. It's funny. It's sad. It's nonsense that somehow makes sense. It's about a little boy who has a fairy godfather with red eyes, a big red nose, and little wings that twitch when he walks. Yet the really strange thing is that this particular fairy godfather really exists! Ladies and gentlemen, meet "Mr. Lupescu."

Vocabulary Preview

ABSTRACT (ab STRAKT) not practical; not
  really existing in fact
  • So far, Ross's career plans are only
  abstract ideas about the future.
FRET (FRET) to be excited with worry.
  • Mom began to *fret* when Roseanne
  wasn't home by midnight.
INTERPRETATION (in TER pruh TAY shun)
  explanation or reason
  • Have you any *interpretation* of Blaine's
  strange behavior?
SOOTHING (SOOTHE ing) comforting,
  calming
  • A Band-Aid and a few *soothing* words
  soon had little Jamie smiling again.
SUSCEPTIBLE (suh SEP tuh bul) open to; likely
  to receive
  • Austin was very *susceptible* to the
  suggestions of his friends.
VAGUE (VAIG) uncertain; not definite
  • I really have only a *vague* idea of the
  kind of career I want.

THE TEACUPS RATTLED, AND FLAMES FLICK-ered over the logs.

"Alan, I *do* wish you could do something about Bobby."

"Isn't that rather Robert's job?"

"Oh you know *Robert*. He's so busy doing good in nice abstract ways with committees in them."

"And headlines."

"He can't be bothered with things like Mr. Lupescu. After all, Bobby's only his *son*."

"And yours, Marjorie."

"And mine. But things like this take a *man*, Alan."

The room was warm and peaceful; Alan stretched his long legs by the fire and felt domestic. Marjorie was soothing even when she fretted. The firelight did things to her hair and the curve of her blouse.

A small whirlwind entered and stopped only when Marjorie said, "Bob-*by!* Say hello nicely to Uncle Alan."

Bobby said hello and stood on one foot.

"Alan . . ." Marjorie prompted.

Alan sat up straight. "Well, Bobby," he said. "And where are you off in such a hurry?"

"See Mr. Lupescu of course. He usually comes afternoons."

"Your mother's been telling me about Mr. Lupescu. He must be quite a person."

"Oh gee I'll say he is, Uncle Alan. He's got a great big red nose and red gloves and red eyes—not like when you've been crying but really red like yours're brown—and little red wings that twitch only he can't fly with them. And he talks like—oh gee I can't do it, but he's swell, he is."

27

"Lupescu's a funny name for a fairy godfather, isn't it, Bobby?"

"Why? Mr. Lupescu always says why do all the fairies have to be Irish because it takes all kinds, doesn't it?"

"*Alan'* Marjorie said. "I don't see that you're doing a *bit* of good. You talk to him seriously like that and you simply make him think it *is* serious. And you *do* know better, don't you, Bobby? You're just joking with us."

"Joking? About *Mr. Lupescu?*"

"Marjorie, you don't— Listen, Bobby. Your mother didn't mean to insult you or Mr. Lupescu. She just doesn't believe in what she's never seen, and you can't blame her. Now, supposing you took her and me out in the garden and we could all see Mr. Lupescu. Wouldn't that be fun?"

"Uh-uh." Bobby shook his head. "Not for Mr. Lupescu. He doesn't like people. Only little boys. And he says if I ever bring people to see him, then he'll let Gorgo get me. G'bye now." And the whirlwind departed.

Marjorie sighed. "At least thank heavens for Gorgo. I never can get a very clear picture out of Bobby, but he says Mr. Lupescu tells the most *terrible* things about him. And if there's any trouble about vegetables or brushing teeth, all I have to say is *Gorgo,* and Bobby does what he's told."

Alan rose. "I don't think you need worry, Marjorie. Mr. Lupescu seems to do more good than harm, and an active imagination is no curse to a child."

"You haven't *lived* with Mr. Lupescu."

"To live in a house like this, I'd chance it," Alan laughed. "But please forgive me now—back to the cottage and the typewriter . . . Seriously, why don't you ask Robert to talk with him?"

Marjorie spread her hands helplessly.

"I know. I'm always the one to assume responsibilities. And yet you married Robert," Alan said.

28

Marjorie laughed. "I don't know. Somehow there's something *about* Robert . . ." Her vague gesture happened to include the original Degas[1] over the fireplace, the sterling tea service,[2] and even the liveried footman[3] who came in at that moment to clear away.

Mr. Lupescu was pretty wonderful that afternoon, all right. He had a little kind of an itch like in his wings and they kept twitching all the time. Stardust, he said. It tickles. Got it up in the Milky Way. Friend of mine has a wagon route up there.

Mr. Lupescu had lots of friends, and they all did something you wouldn't ever think of, not in a squillion years. That's why he didn't like people, because people don't do things you can tell stories about. They just work or keep house or are mothers or something.

But one of Mr. Lupescu's friends, now, was captain of a ship, only it went in time, and Mr. Lupescu took trips with him and came back and told you all about what was happening this very minute five hundred years ago. And another of the friends was a radio engineer, only he could tune in on all the kingdoms and Mr. Lupescu would squidgle up his red nose and twist it like a dial and make noises like all the kingdoms coming in on the set. And then there was Gorgo, only he wasn't a friend—not exactly; not even to Mr. Lupescu.

They'd been playing for a couple of weeks—only it must've been really hours, cause Mamselle[4] hadn't yelled about supper yet, but Mr. Lupescu says Time is funny—

---

[1] *Degas* (day GAH)—Edgar Degas (1834-1917), a French painter. An original painting by Degas would be very expensive.
[2] *sterling tea service* (STIR ling TEA SUR VIS)—silver tray, sugar bowl, teapot, and cream pitcher used to serve tea.
[3] *liveried* (LIV uh rid) *footman*—a servant in a uniform.
[4] *Mamselle* (mam ZEL)—an informal name for the maid.

29

when Mr. Lupescu screwed up his red eyes and said, "Bobby, let's go in the house."

"But there's people in the house, and you don't—"

"I know I don't like people. That's why we're going in the house. Come on, Bobby, or I'll—"

So what could you do when you didn't even want to hear him say Gorgo's name?

He went into Father's study,[5] and it was a strict rule that nobody *ever* went into Father's study, but rules weren't for Mr. Lupescu.

Father was on the telephone telling somebody he'd try to be at a luncheon but there was a committee meeting that same morning but he'd see. While he was talking, Mr. Lupescu went over to a table and opened a drawer and took something out.

When Father hung up, he saw Bobby first and started to be very mad. He said, "Young man, you've been trouble enough to your Mother and me with all your stories about your red-winged Mr. Lupescu, and now if you're to start bursting in—"

You have to be polite and introduce people. "Father, this is Mr. Lupescu. And see, he does too have red wings."

Mr. Lupescu held out the gun he'd taken from the drawer and shot Father once right through the forehead. It made a little clean hole in front and a big messy hole in back. Father fell down and was dead.

"Now, Bobby," Mr. Lupescu said, "a lot of people are going to come here and ask you a lot of questions. And if you don't tell the truth about exactly what happened, I'll send Gorgo to fetch you."

Then Mr. Lupescu was gone.

"It's a curious case, Lieutenant," the medical examiner

[5] *study* (STUD ee)—a home office or den.

said. I can at least give you a lead until you get the experts in. The child's statement that his fairy godfather shot his father is obviously susceptible of two interpretations. A, the father shot himself; the child was so horrified by the sight that he refused to accept it and invented this explanation. B, the child shot the father, let us say by accident, and shifted the blame to his imaginary scapegoat.[6] If the child had resented his father and created an ideal substitute, he might make the substitute destroy the reality. . . .

The man with the red nose and eyes and gloves and wings walked down the back lane to the cottage. As soon as he got inside, he took off his coat and removed his wings and the strings and rubber that made them twitch. He laid them on top of the ready pile of kindling and lit the fire. When it was well started, he added the gloves. Then he took off the nose, jammed it into a crack in the wall, and smoothed it over. Then he took the red contact lenses out of his brown eyes and went into the kitchen, found a hammer, pounded them to powder, and washed the powder down the sink.

Alan started to pour himself a drink and found, to his pleased surprise, that he didn't especially need one. But he did feel tired. He could lie down and recapitulate it all, from the invention of Mr. Lupescu (and Gorgo and the man with the Milky Way route) to today's success and on into the future when Marjorie—trusting Marjorie—would be more desirable than ever as Robert's widow and heir. And Bobby would need a *man* to look after him.

Alan went into the bedroom. Several years passed by in the few seconds it took him to recognize what was waiting on the bed, but then, Time is funny.

Alan said nothing.

"Mr. Lupescu, I presume?" said Gorgo.

[6] scapegoat (SKAPE gote)—a person who bears blame for others.

Recall

1. At the beginning of the story, Bobby (a) is quite sure that Mr. Lupescu really exists (b) enjoys telling lies about Mr. Lupescu (c) probably knows who Mr. Lupescu really is.
2. When Alan seems to take Mr. Lupescu seriously, it makes Marjorie (a) fearful for Bobby's life (b) secretly pleased (c) disappointed.
3. Alan has to take Mr. Lupescu seriously because (a) he has also been visited by Mr. Lupescu in private (b) Alan too is terrified of Gorgo (c) Mr. Lupescu is part of Alan's plan to murder Robert.
4. One truly amazing thing about Mr. Lupescu is that he can (a) be in two places at once (b) travel in time (c) travel in space.
5. The "something" that Mr. Lupescu takes from the table drawer turns out to be (a) an artificial nose (b) a telephone (c) a gun.
6. Except for Bobby, the one person in the story who sees Mr. Lupescu standing in front of him is (a) Robert (b) Alan (c) Marjorie.
7. The medical examiner explains that Bobby may have (a) disliked and shot his father (b) dressed up like Mr. Lupescu (c) planned the whole thing.
8. The medical examiner offers two explanations, both of which are (a) right (b) probably right (c) wrong.
9. The eyes, wings, and nose are destroyed or hidden because (a) Mr. Lupescu has served his purpose (b) Mr. Lupescu has decided to travel (c) Bobby no longer believes in Mr. Lupescu.
10. Amazingly enough, the character waiting on the bed to greet Alan at the end of the story is (a) Mr. Lupescu (b) Robert (c) Gorgo.

32

Infer

11. One word in the story that can't be found in a dictionary is *squillion* ("not in a squillion years"). It probably means (a) hundred (b) thousand (c) an impossibly large number.

12. Another word in the story can't be found in a dictionary: "Mr. Lupeseu could *squidgle* up his red nose." *Squidgle* probably means (a) light (b) wrinkle into a tight ball (c) poke something soft.

13. The character who has a secret in the first scene of the story is (a) Bobby (b) Marjorie (c) Alan.

14. Many clues in the story indicate that Robert, the husband, is (a) a man of action (b) very rich (c) dissatisfied with his marriage.

15. The crime was planned by (a) Alan and Marjorie (b) Alan alone (c) the evil Gorgo.

16. Alan seems to earn his living as a (a) professional criminal (b) writer (c) committee member.

17. Alan is also a very good (a) painter (b) musician (c) actor.

18. Alan commits his crime because of his desire for (a) fame and money (b) love and fame (c) love and money.

19. Which of the following groups of words refers to the same person? (a) Bobby's uncle, Alan, Gorgo (b) Mr. Lupescu, Alan, Gorgo (c) Mr. Lupescu, Bobby's uncle, Alan.

20. The story illustrates the old idea of the (a) perfect crime (b) trickster tricked (c) lovers' quarrel.

Vocabulary Review

1. If you are *susceptible* to colds you probably (a) catch cold easily (b) seldom catch cold (c) don't really mind colds.

2. If someone says, "The President's speech last night was too *abstract*," he means that the speech was (a) dishonest (b) lacking in definite suggestions (c) full of details.
3. Another word that means almost the same thing as *abstract* in the above sentence is (a) *domestic* (b) *soothing* (c) *vague*.
4. "Marjorie was *soothing* even when she *fretted*." In other words, Marjorie was (a) calming even when she talked too much (b) comforting even when she worried (c) singing even as she played the guitar.
5. An *interpretation* of a dream is the same thing as (a) a memory (b) a nightmare (c) an explanation.

Critical Thinking

1. One way in which we can see that the writer has done a good job is that certain lines turn out to have meanings that are not obvious at first. Explain how each of the following *italicized* lines gains in meaning as the story continues:
   (a) Marjorie: "You haven't *lived* with Mr. Lupescu."
   Alan: *"To live in a house like this, I'd chance it."*
   (b) Bobby: "But there's people in the house, and you don't—"
   Mr. Lupescu: *"I know I don't like people. That's why we're going in the house."*
2. How old is Bobby? Explain your answer.
3. Not all readers take the end of the story in the same way. Explain your *interpretation* of the appearance of Gorgo.

Test

Theodore L. Thomas

*Don't let the title set you off. "Test" isn't a school
exam or a scientific experiment. "Test" is simply
one of the most thrilling science fiction stories ever
written. Reading it is like taking a trip on a roller
coaster. First you're pulled slowly to the top. You
breathe deeply and enjoy the view. Then you start
down—down—around—around in a wild ride that
ends in two loop the loops. Your heart's in your
throat. Your brain's limp from a double twist that
leaves you reeling. Somehow, the trip's a joy.
Hang on tight. Here we go!*

Vocabulary Preview

ABREAST (uh BREST) beside; even with
- The bus pulled *abreast* of the car and then passed it.

CAREEN (kuh REEN) to cause to lurch or lean to one side
- Maria managed to miss hitting the tree by *careening* her sled to the left.

CONSCIOUSNESS (KON shus nis) the state of being conscious, or awake and aware
- Roy felt himself fainting; then he lost *consciousness.*

FATIGUE (fuh TEEG) extreme tiredness; a very exhausted condition
- After the twenty-mile march, the soldiers felt only *fatigue* and hunger.

MOMENTUM (moe MEN tum) force of motion in a moving object
- Mindy put on the brakes, but the *momentum* of her big car carried it into the fence.

SUSTAIN (suh STAIN) to keep up or hold up
- A racehorse cannot *sustain* its top speed for very long.

WRENCH (RENCH) a sudden hard twist
- Luis gave his ankle a *wrench* when he fell on the stairs.

Robert Proctor was a good driver for so young a man. The Turnpike curved gently ahead of him, lightly travelled on this cool morning in May. He felt relaxed and alert. Two hours of driving had not yet produced the fatigue that appeared first in the muscles in the base of the neck. The sun was bright, but not glaring, and the air smelled fresh and clean. He breathed it deeply, and blew it out noisily. It was a good day for driving.

He glanced quickly at the slim, grey-haired woman sitting in the front seat with him. Her mouth was curved in a quiet smile. She watched the trees and the fields slip by on her side of the pike. Robert Proctor immediately looked back at the road. He said, "Enjoying it, Mom?"

"Yes, Robert." Her voice was as cool as the morning. "It is very pleasant to sit here. I was thinking of the driving I did for you when you were little. I wonder if you enjoyed it as much as I enjoy this."

He smiled, embarrassed. "Sure I did."

She reached over and patted him gently on the arm, and then turned back to the scenery.

He listened to the smooth purr of the engine. Up ahead he saw a great truck, spouting smoke as it sped along the Turnpike. Behind it, not passing it, was a long blue convertible. Robert Proctor noted the arrangement and filed it in the back of his mind. He was slowly overtaking them, but he would not reach them for another minute or two.

He listened to the purr of the engine, and he was pleased

37

with the sound. He had tuned that engine himself over the objections of the mechanic. The engine idled rough now, but it ran smoothly at high speed. You needed a special feel to do good work on engines, and Robert Proctor knew he had it. No one in the world had a feel like his for the tune of an engine.

It was a good morning for driving, and his mind was filled with good thoughts. He pulled nearly abreast of the blue convertible and began to pass it. His speed was a few miles per hour above the Turnpike limit, but his car was under perfect control. The blue convertible suddenly swung out from behind the truck. It swung out without warning and struck his car near the right front fender, knocking his car to the shoulder on the left of the Turnpike lane.

Robert Proctor was a good driver, too wise to slam on the brakes. He fought the steering wheel to hold the car on a straight path. The left wheels sank into the soft left shoulder, and the car tugged to pull to the left and cross the island and enter the lanes carrying the cars heading in the opposite direction. He held it, then the wheel struck a rock buried in the soft dirt, and the left front tire blew out. It was then that his mother began to scream.

The car turned sideways and skidded part of the way out into the other lanes. Robert Proctor fought against the steering wheel to straighten the car, but the drag of the blown tire was too much. The scream rang steadily in his ears, and even as he strained at the wheel one part of his mind wondered coolly how a scream could so long be sustained without a breath. An oncoming car struck his radiator from the side and spun him full into the left-hand lanes.

He was flung into his mother's lap, and she was thrown against the right door. It held. With his left hand he reached for the steering wheel and pulled himself erect against the force of the spin. He turned the wheel to the left, and tried to stop the spin and career out of the lanes of oncoming traffic. His mother was unable to right herself; she lay against the door, her cry rising and falling with the spin of the car.

The car lost some of its momentum. During one of the spins he twisted the wheel straight, and the car wobblingly stopped spinning and headed down the lane. Before Robert Proctor could turn it off the pike to safety a car loomed ahead of him, bearing down on him. There was a man at the wheel of that other car, sitting rigid, unable to move, eyes wide and staring and filled with fright. Alongside the man was a girl, her head against the back of the seat, soft curls framing a lovely face, her eyes closed in easy sleep. It was not the fear in the man that reached into Robert Proctor; it was the trusting helplessness in the face of the sleeping girl. The two cars sped closer to each other, and Robert Proctor could not change the direction of his car. The driver of the other car remained frozen at the wheel. At the last moment Robert Proctor sat motionless staring into the face of the onrushing, sleeping girl, his mother's cry still sounding in his ears. He heard no crash when the two cars collided head-on at a high rate of speed. He felt something push into his stomach, and the world began to go grey. Just before he lost consciousness he heard the scream stop, and he knew then that he had been hearing a single, short-lived scream that had only seemed to drag on and on. There came a painless wrench, and then darkness.

Robert Proctor seemed to be at the bottom of a deep black well. There was a spot of faint light in the far distance, and he could hear the rumble of a distant voice. He tried to pull himself toward the light and the sound, but the effort was too great. He lay still and gathered himself and tried again. The light grew brighter and the voice louder. He tried harder, again, and he drew closer. Then he opened his eyes full and looked at the man sitting in front of him.

"You all right, Son?" asked the man. He wore a blue uniform, and his round, beefy face was familiar.

Robert Proctor moved his head, and discovered he was seated in a chair, unharmed, and able to move his arms and legs with no trouble. He looked around the room, and he remembered.

The man in the uniform saw the growing intelligence in his eyes and he said, "No harm done, Son. You just took the last part of your driver's test."

Robert Proctor focused his eyes on the man. Though he saw the man clearly, he seemed to see the faint face of the sleeping girl in front of him.

The uniformed man continued to speak. "We put you through an accident under hypnosis—do it to everybody these days before they can get their driver's licenses. Makes better drivers of them, more careful drivers the rest of their lives. Remember it now? Coming in here and all?"

Robert Proctor nodded, thinking of the sleeping girl. She never would have awakened; she would have passed right from a sweet, temporary sleep into the dark heavy sleep of death, nothing in between. His mother would have been bad enough; after all, she was pretty old. The sleeping girl was downright waste.

The uniformed man was still speaking. "So you're all set now. You pay me the ten dollar fee, and sign this application, and we'll have your license in the mail in a day or two." He did not look up.

Robert Proctor placed a ten dollar bill on the table in front of him, glanced over the application and signed it. He looked up to find two white-uniformed men, standing one on each side of him, and he frowned in annoyance. He started to speak, but the uniformed man, spoke first. "Sorry, Son. You failed. You're sick; you need treatment."

The two men lifted Robert Proctor to his feet, and he said, "Take your hands off me. What is this?"

The uniformed man said, "Nobody should want to drive a car after going through what you just went through. It should take months before you can even think of driving again, but you're ready right now. Killing people doesn't bother you. We don't let your kind run around loose in society any more. But don't you worry now, Son. They'll take good care of you, and they'll fix you up." He nodded to the two men, and they began to march Robert Proctor out.

At the door he spoke, and his voice was so urgent the two men paused. Robert Proctor said, "You can't really mean this. I'm still dreaming, aren't I? This is still part of the test, isn't it?"

The uniformed man said, *"How do any of us know?"* And they dragged Robert Proctor out the door, knees stiff, feet dragging, his rubber heels sliding along the two grooves worn into the floor.

Recall

1. The opening statement that Robert Proctor was "a good driver" is later proven to be true by (a) the way he keeps his feelings under control (b) his handling of the car in an emergency (c) his accident-free driving record.

2. Just before and after the crash, Robert Proctor felt worst about (a) the driver of the other car (b) the sleeping girl (c) himself.

3. The second part of the story takes place (a) in a hospital (b) on a highway (c) in a driver's license office.

41

4. The accident turns out to have been (a) a test under hypnosis (b) a bad dream (c) a frightening movie.

5. Robert Proctor is told that he failed the test because (a) he was unable to avoid the other car (b) his application contained spelling errors (c) he didn't feel disturbed enough about the accident.

Infer

6. Several things in the story indicate that Robert Proctor is about (a) eighteen (b) thirty (c) forty-five.

7. The accident—as described—was mostly the fault of (a) Robert Proctor (b) the driver of the blue convertible (c) the driver beside the sleeping girl.

8. In truth, the scream of Robert Proctor's mother (a) lasted many minutes (b) actually came from Robert Proctor's throat (c) was quite short.

9. The "two white-uniformed men" at the end of the story were probably from a (a) police station (b) mental hospital (c) car-washing company.

10. The last sentence of the story tells us that (a) many other people had failed the test (b) Robert Proctor was the first to fail (c) in a few days Robert Proctor would be perfectly happy.

Vocabulary Review

Write on your paper the word in *italics* that belongs in each blank. Use each word only once.

abreast	*fatigue*	*sustain*
careen	*momentum*	*wrench*
consciousness	*spouting*	

1. A person under hypnosis does not have what we usually consider to be total ———.

2. If you were forced to ——— a walking speed of five miles an hour for five hours, you would feel a lot of ———.

3. The ——— of the huge bus made it ——— crazily when it struck the ice.

4. The cat gave the mouse's neck a hard ———, and soon the little animal was spouting blood.

5. The path was too narrow for two people to walk ———.

Critical Thinking

1. Although "Test" is a fast-moving action story, it starts slowly and peacefully. Why do you think the author chose to begin in such a calm and relaxed way?

2. Nothing in the story indicates exactly when it is supposed to happen. In your opinion, could it happen this year in a state or provincial office for drivers' licenses? Why, or why not? If you think it is supposed to happen in the future, just how far in the future? Explain.

3. Have you ever been in a bad accident that you saw coming just before it happened? If so, you know that one thing in "Test" is absolutely true. Between the time you see that an accident will happen and the time it actually occurs, seconds *do* seem like minutes. Mrs. Proctor's short scream *could* have seemed to "drag on and on." What do you think causes this?

4. Find the paragraph that starts " 'You all right, Son?' " on page 40. When you first read these four words, whom did you think was the speaker? Why? Discuss your answer with other readers of the story.

5. Suppose that all people who now hold drivers' licenses could be retested as described in "Test." Suppose also that this new testing would result in half the drivers losing their licenses *and* half the accidents being avoided. Do you think such a retesting program would be a good idea? Why, or why not?

6. Think again about the sentence in *italics* near the end of the story: " 'How do any of us know?' " What does it mean to you? What might the author be trying to point out?

The Oval Portrait

Edgar Allan Poe

There's really nothing new about science
fiction and fantasy. Every country, in every age,
has had its own favorite stories. Thousands of
years ago, the ancient Greeks were telling each
other about men who put on wings to fly through
the air. The Africans of old had a story about a
person who built a tower to climb to the moon. Old
Europe had its "evil eyes" and its werewolves.
And later, here in America, we had our famous
Fountain of Youth. We also had writers like Edgar
Allan Poe (1809-1849), the author of such delicious
horrors as "The Tell-Tale Heart," "The Fall of the
House of Usher," and the very short "Oval
Portrait." Shiver silently, please.

Vocabulary Preview

ABANDONED (uh BAN dund) deserted; given up and left empty
  • The old house on the corner was *abandoned* several years ago.

FAWN (FAWN) a young deer
  • The mother deer hid the *fawn* in some bushes.

GRANDEUR (GRAN jur) greatness
  • I'll never forget the *grandeur* of New York's big buildings.

RADIANT (RAY dee unt) bright; beaming
  • The child's face was *radiant* with joy.

RIVAL (RIE vul) a competitor; a person who tries to win over another
  • Mindy's only real *rival* in the race was Sondra Walsh.

TAPESTRY (TAP ih stree) a picture or design woven into cloth and used as a wall hanging
  • A huge *tapestry* covered the wall behind the king's bed.

WITHERED (WITH urd) dried up; shriveled
  • The hot sun *withered* the wild flowers Jason had picked.

M Y SERVANT AND I FORCED OUR WAY

into the old castle. It was one of those piles of gloom and grandeur that have long frowned among the mountains of Europe. I was wounded. So it was a better place to pass a night than in the open air. The castle appeared to have been only recently abandoned.

We settled into one of the smaller apartments. It lay in a distant tower of the building. Its decorations were rich, yet tattered and old. Its walls were hung with tapestry. There were a great number of modern paintings in frames of rich gold. These paintings hung not only on the larger walls but in the many nooks and corners. I took a great interest in these paintings, perhaps due to my excited state of mind.

I told Pedro to close the heavy curtains at the windows. It was already night. I told him to light the tongues in the tall candles that stood by the head of my bed, and to throw open the heavy black curtains that surrounded the bed. I wanted to study the pictures and read a small notebook I found on the pillow. The notebook told the history of the paintings.

Long, long I read—and long, long I gazed. The hours flew by. Deep midnight came. The position of the candle holder displeased me. I reached out with difficulty. I placed it so that it would throw more light upon the pages.

But the action had an effect I had not expected. The light of the many candles (for there *were* many) now fell upon a previously hidden nook. I thus saw in clear light a picture I had not noticed before. It was the portrait of a lovely girl, almost a woman. I glanced at the painting hurriedly. I then closed my eyes. I do not know why I did this. I ran over in my mind my reason for shutting them. It was a sudden movement to gain time for thought. I wanted to make sure my eyes were not fooling me. I wanted to calm my imagination for a more careful look. In a few moments I again looked at the painting.

The portrait was that of a lovely girl. It was a head-and-shoulders painting. Something artists call a *vignette*. The arms, the head, and even the ends of the radiant hair melted softly into the vague shadows of the background. The frame was oval. It was richly covered with gold. I had never seen a finer painting. Yet it was not the skill of the painter nor the beauty of the face that excited me. Nor had my imagination mistaken the head for that of a living person. I knew that it was a painting. I lay for an hour, half sitting, half lying down with my eyes always on the portrait.

At length I fell back into the bed. I understood what had alarmed me. I had found the portrait to be *absolutely lifelike*. It wasn't just a picture! It was the girl herself! This fact first startled me, then amazed me, then confused me. I had a deep sense of wonder. I replaced the candle holder to its former position. The painting was shut from view. I reached for the notebook that discussed the history of the paintings. I turned to the section on the oval portrait. I there read the strange words that follow:

She was a maiden of the rarest beauty. She was as full of happiness as she was beautiful. Evil was the day when she saw the painter. And evil was the day when she loved and wedded him. He loved his art and could not love another.

She was all light and smiles. She was as playful as a fawn. She loved all things except the Art that was her rival. She dreaded the paints and brushes and other things that deprived her of the face and friendship of her lover. It was thus a terrible thing for her to hear the artist speak of his desire to paint his young bride.

Because she was sweet and obedient, she sat

48

sweetly for many weeks. She sat in the high dark tower room. The light dripped in only from a single window overhead. She longed for the out-of-doors. But he, the painter, took glory in his work. He went on from hour to hour, from day to day. He was excited, and wild, and moody. He became lost in his own thoughts and did not think of his bride.

The artist would not see that the light that fell from the single window was withering the health and spirits of his bride. She looked worse and worse to all but him.

Yet she smiled without complaining, because she saw how much the painter took a pleasure in his job. She loved him, yet grew daily weaker and weaker. Some people who saw the portrait thought it was proof that the artist loved her. He painted her surprisingly well. They talked in low words of its lifelike beauty.

At length, as the work drew to a close, the artist allowed no other people to the tower. For the painter had grown wild with the love of his work. He rarely turned his eyes from the portrait. He rarely looked at the face of his wife. He would not see that the colors that he spread upon the portrait were drawn from the cheeks of her who sat beside him.

Many weeks had passed. Little remained to do. There was only one brush upon the mouth and one spot of color upon the eye. The spirit of the lady leaped up, like the flame in a dying candle. And then the artist applied the brush. The spot was placed.

For one moment the artist stood spellbound before the portrait he had painted. In the next moment, still gazing at the portrait, the artist began to shake and grow very pale. He cried out in a loud voice, "This is indeed Life itself!" He turned suddenly to look at his wife. *She was dead!*

49

Recall

1. The narrator (person who tells the story) took shelter in the old castle because he was (a) curious about the inside (b) wounded (c) alone at night.
2. The narrator did not notice the oval portrait at first because (a) it was in a dark corner (b) he hadn't yet read the interesting story in the notebook (c) it was covered by a tapestry.
3. The narrator makes it clear that what excited him most about the portrait was (a) the skill of the painter (b) the beauty of the girl (c) its lifelikeness.
4. The painter loved (a) money more than art (b) the portrait more than his wife (c) death more than life.
5. At the end of the story, the girl is alive (a) in the picture only (b) in both real life and the picture (c) only in the painter's imagination.

Infer

6. The setting (place) of the story (a) makes the tale seem real because most readers have lived in similar places (b) matters not at all (c) adds to the air of mystery.
7. The narrator is correctly described as being (a) somewhat excited, but in control of himself (b) excited beyond all control (c) completely out of his mind.
8. The narrator states that he told his servant to "light the tongues in the tall candle holder. . . ." The word *tongues* probably means (a) fire tongs (b) the wicks of candles (c) hissing gas lamps.

9. The author of the notebook seems to praise the young woman for being modest, obedient, and sweet. This is one reason for believing that the story tells of events happening (a) in the past (b) at the present (c) in some future time.

10. The author's purpose in writing the story was probably to (a) report on an event from his own life (b) explain a scientific fact (c) cause his readers to shiver and shake.

Vocabulary Review

On your paper, write the *italicized* word that belongs in each blank.

abandoned	*grandeur*	*rival*
fawn	*radiant*	*tapestry*
		withered

1. A *withered* face would probably not be ——————.
2. The opposite of an occupied house is a(n) —————— house.
3. A cloth wall hanging that has detailed pictures might be called a ——————.
4. The opposite of *plainness* or *simplicity* is ——————.
5. In a game of solitaire, your only —————— is the game itself.

Critical Thinking

1. What are the three most important words you can think of to describe the painter? What are the three most important words for the girl? the narrator? Explain how each of your words tells something absolutely necessary to the story.

51

2. In a way, "The Oval Portrait" is two stories: (1) an "outer" story about the narrator, and (2) an "inner" story about the painter and the girl. The inner story is certainly the more important. In fact, the author could have told it by itself, without the outer story at all. Why do you think Edgar Allan Poe chose to add the outer story? How does it help to have the tale of the painter and the girl come from a notebook found by the narrator?

3. Unlike some stories in this book, "The Oval Portrait" could have really happened. Explain how the story has both a natural and a supernatural explanation.

The Perfect Woman

Robert Sheckley

FOR MEN ONLY: *What's your idea of the perfect woman?*
FOR WOMEN ONLY: *What's your idea of the perfect man?*

The answer to both questions is probably the same: a person who's thoughtful, loving, even tempered, kind, good looking, intelligent, forgiving, practical, farsighted, amusing, hard working, strong in the right beliefs. . . . and so on.

But whatever your idea, as things stand now it's only an idea. Human beings are human beings. No person is perfect. Suppose, however, that in the world of the future, men could create "perfect" women, or women create "perfect" men. Do you think you'd actually be happy with such a mate? Would life with a "perfect" husband or wife really be the best possible life? The story that follows suggests an answer.

53

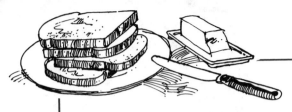

Vocabulary Preview

PRIMITIVE (PRIM uh tiv) of the earliest times; simple and crude, as in early times
  • *Primitive* men and women lived in caves and hunted for food.

PRIMITIVIST (PRIM uh tiv ist) a person who knows about and admires the primitive way of life.
  • Mrs. Watson is a *primitivist* who thinks modern life too complicated.

RALLIED (RAL eed) improved suddenly in health
  • My grandmother *rallied* about midnight and is now expected to live.

REACTION TIME (ree AK shun TIME) the time it takes a person to react or respond to something.
  • A good boxer must have split-second *reaction time.*

REFLEXES (Rih flek sez) reactions; responses to something from outside
  • Miguel's *reflexes* are so fast that he can catch flies with one hand.

RESPONSIVE (rih SPON siv) quick to react or respond to something
  • The *responsive* class quickly answered the teacher's questions.

Mr. MORCHECK AWOKE WITH A SOUR taste in his mouth and a laugh ringing in his ears. It was George Owen-Clark's laugh, the last thing he remembered from the Triad-Morgan party. And what a party it had been! All Earth had been celebrating the turn of the century. The year Three Thousand! Peace and prosperity to all, and happy life. . . .

"How happy is your life?" Owen-Clark had asked, grinning slyly, more than a little drunk. "I mean, how is life with your sweet wife?"

That had been unpleasant. Everyone knew that Owen-Clark was a Primitivist, but what right had he to rub people's noses in it? Just because he had married a Primitive Woman. . . .

"I love my wife," Morcheck had said firmly. "And she's a hell of a lot nicer and more responsive than that bundle of nerves you call *your* wife."

But of course, you can't get under the thick hide of a Primitivist. Primitivists love the faults in their women as much as their good points—more, perhaps. Owen-Clark had grinned ever more slyly, and said, "You know, Morcheck old man, I think your wife needs a checkup. Have you noticed her reflexes lately?"

What an idiot! Mr. Morcheck eased himself out of bed, blinking at the bright morning sun which hid behind his

55

curtains. Myra's reflexes—the hell of it was, there was a germ of truth in what Owen-Clark had said. Of late, Myra had seemed rather—out of sorts.

"Myra!" Morcheck called. "Is my coffee ready?" There was a pause. Then her voice floated brightly upstairs. "In a minute!"

Morcheck slid into a pair of slacks, still blinking sleepily. Thank Stat the next three days were celebration-points. He'd need all of them just to get over last night's party.

Downstairs, Myra was hurrying around, pouring coffee, folding napkins, pulling out his chair for him. He sat down, and she kissed him on his bald spot. He liked being kissed on his bald spot.

"How's my little wife this morning?" he asked.

"Wonderful, darling," she said after a little pause. "I made Seffiners for you this morning. You like Seffiners."

Morcheck bit into one, done to a turn, and sipped his coffee.

"How do you feel this morning?" he asked her.

Myra buttered a piece of toast for him, then said, "Wonderful, darling. You know, it was a perfectly wonderful party last night. I loved every moment of it."

"I got a bit veery," Morcheck said with a half grin.

"I love you when you're veery," Myra said. "You talk like an angel—like a very clever angel, I mean. I could listen to you forever." She buttered another piece of toast for him.

Mr. Morcheck smiled at her like a friendly sun, then frowned. He put down his Seffiner and scratched his cheek. "You know," he said, "I had a little run-in with Owen-Clark. He was talking about Primitive Women."

Myra buttered a fifth piece of toast for him without answering, adding it to the growing pile. She started to reach for a sixth, but he touched her hand lightly. She bent forward and kissed him on the nose.

"Primitive Women!" she exclaimed. "Those neurotic creatures! Aren't you happier with me, dear? I may be Modern—but no Primitive Woman could love you the way I do—and I adore you!"

What she said was true. Man had never, in all history, been able to live happily with a real Primitive Woman. The selfish, spoiled creatures demanded a lifetime of care and attention. It was terrible that Owen-Clark's wife made him dry the dishes. And the fool put up with it! Primitive Women were forever asking for money with which to buy clothes, demanding breakfast in bed, dashing off to bridge games, talking for hours on the telephone, and Stat knows what else. They tried to take over men's jobs. In this way, they proved their equality.

Some idiots like Owen-Clark insisted on their excellence.

Under his wife's care and love, Mr. Morcheck felt his hangover melt slowly away. Myra wasn't eating. He knew that she had eaten earlier, so that she could give her full attention to feeding him. It was little things like that that made all the difference.

"He said your reaction time had slowed down."

"He did?" Myra asked, after a pause. "Those Primitivists think they know everything."

It was the right answer, but it had taken too long. Mr. Morcheck asked his wife a few more questions, checking her reaction time by the second hand on the kitchen clock. She *was* slowing up!

"Did the mail come?" he asked her quickly. "Did anyone call? Will I be late for work?"

After three seconds she opened her mouth, then closed it again. Something was terribly wrong.

"I love you," she said simply.

Mr. Morcheck felt his heart pound against his ribs. He loved her! Madly, passionately! But that disgusting Owen-

Clark had been right. She needed a checkup. Myra seemed to sense his thought. She rallied a little, and said, "All I want is your happiness, dear. I think I'm sick. . . . Will you have me cured? Will you take me back after I'm cured—and not let them change me—I wouldn't want to be changed!" Her bright head sank on her arms. She cried—noiselessly, so as not to disturb him.

"It'll just be a checkup, darling," Morcheck said, trying to hold back his own tears. But he knew—as well as she knew—that she was really sick.

It was so unfair, he thought. Primitive Woman, with her old-fashioned brain and body, was almost never in poor health. But delicate Modern Woman was something else again. So unfair! Because Modern Woman contained all the finest, dearest qualities a woman could have.

Except the ability to keep going.

Myra rallied again. She raised herself to her feet with an effort. She was very beautiful. Her sickness had put a high color in her cheeks, and the morning sun brightened her hair.

"My darling," she said. "Won't you let me stay a little longer? I may recover by myself." But her eyes were fast becoming clouded.

"Darling . . ." She caught herself quickly, holding on to an edge of the table. "When you have a new wife—try to remember how much I loved you." She sat down, her face blank.

"I'll get the car," Morcheck murmured, and hurried away. Any longer and he would have broken down himself.

Walking to the garage he felt numb, tired, broken. Myra —gone! And modern science, for all its wonders, unable to help.

He reached the garage and said, "All right, back out." Smoothly his car backed out and stopped beside him.

"Anything wrong, boss?" his car asked. "You look worried. Still got a hangover?"

"No—it's Myra. She's sick."

The car was silent for a moment. Then it said softly, "I'm very sorry, Mr. Morcheck. I wish there were something I could do."

"Thank you," Morcheck said, glad to have a friend at this hour. "I'm afraid there's nothing anyone can do."

The car backed to the door and Morcheck helped Myra inside. Gently the car started.

It maintained a polite silence on the way back to the factory.

Recall

1. The story is supposed to happen (a) on January 1, 3000 (b) in our lifetimes (c) three thousand years from today.
2. George Owen-Clark, the Primitivist at the party, (a) wanted a wife like Myra (b) flirted only with Modern Women (c) loved his wife's faults as well as her good points.
3. Mr. Morcheck begins to agree with Owen-Clark that (a) Primitive Women are superior (b) Modern Women are superior (c) Myra's reflexes are slowing down.
4. During breakfast, Myra (a) acts like a Primitive Woman (b) eats as much as Morcheck (c) waits on Morcheck like a maid.

5. Morcheck thinks that Modern Women lack only one thing: (a) beauty (b) interest in preparing good meals (c) the ability to keep going.
6. The story ends with Myra (a) on her way to an automobile assembly plant (b) going back to the factory (c) taking Morcheck to his factory job.

Infer

7. One word in the story can't be found in the dictionary: *Stat* ("Thank Stat . . .," ". . . and Stat knows what else"). *Stat* seems to be a future substitute for the word (a) communism (b) God (c) woman.
8. The two words that best describe Myra are (a) independent and creative (b) selfish and mistrustful (c) obedient and adoring.
9. The author suggests that for many men, life with a Modern Woman might be (a) confusing (b) perfect (c) horrible in every respect.
10. The introduction of the talking car at the end of the story suggests that by the year 3000 (a) men love their cars (b) everyone has his own car (c) a great many changes have taken place.

Vocabulary Review

Write on your paper the term in *italics* that belongs in each blank. Use each term only once.

primitive   *reaction time*
primitivist   *reflexes*
rallied   *responsive*

1. Champion ping-pong players must have good —————
   and —————.
2. People who are cooperative and quick with others are said
   to be —————.
3. A football team that comes from way behind to win in the
   fourth quarter has certainly —————.
4. A ————— is a person who is interested in the ways
   of ————— human beings.

Critical Thinking

1. The character Morcheck approves of Modern Women. It's
quite clear that author Robert Sheckley does not. Exactly
what does the author suggest is wrong with Modern
Women? Why might life with a Primitive Woman be more
interesting? Explain.

2. *Modern Women are not really women because they're not
really people.* Explain this statement. Then find sentences
from the story that support it.

3. The talking car at the end of the story strikes most readers
as a complete surprise. Why do you think the author added
the car? In what ways are the car and Myra similar?

61

4. Many people today believe strongly in the Women's Liberation movement. They would probably like the fact that this story suggests that the male dream of the "perfect wife" is as laughable as it is impossible. Is there anything a strong supporter of women's rights might *dislike* about the story? Think carefully.

The Mathematicians

Arthur Feldman

How old will you be in the year 2005? That's a very important date. According to the story that follows, 2005 is when the earth will be attacked by creatures from outer space. They'll come not from Mars or Venus, but from the "Dog Star" Sirius, the brightest star in the sky. And they'll come not in space ships but on bright green wings. They'll be much smarter than human beings. They'll all know mathematics. They'll master our languages quickly. Do you think human beings will have much of a chance.

Maybe you think all this is nonsense. Not at all!

Remember, it's Sirius.

Vocabulary Preview

ENSLAVE (en SLAVE) to make slaves of
  • The creatures from outer space quickly *enslaved* the earth's people.

HAMMOCK (HAM uk) a piece of cloth or netting hung between two supports and used as a bed
  • Right now I'd like to be lying in a *hammock* under a cool shade tree.

INVADER (in VADE er) a person or group that enters another country by force
  • In World War II, the Germans were the *invaders* of France.

ORGAN (OR gun) a part of the body that has a special function, or duty
  • Is the heart the most important *organ* in the body?

PERSUASION (per SWAY zhun) the ability to persuade or convince
  • Bill's *persuasion* finally led me to stop smoking.

SAINTLINESS (SAINT lee nes) the quality of being a saintly or unusually fine person
  • Midge's *saintliness* is amazing because her sisters are like little devils.

THEY WERE IN THE GARDEN. "NOW, ZOE," said Zenia Hawkins to her nine-year-old daughter, "quit fluttering around, and papa will tell you a story."

Zoe settled down in the hammock. "A true story, papa?"

"It all happened exactly as I'm going to tell you," said Drake Hawkins, pinching Zoe's rosy cheek. "Now: two thousand and eleven years ago in A.D. 2005—figuring by the calendar used at that time—a tribe of beings from the Dog Star, Sirius, invaded the earth."

"And what did these beings look like, father?"

"Like humans in many, many ways. They each had two arms, two legs, and all the other organs."

"Wasn't there any difference at all between the Star beings and the humans, papa?"

"There was. The newcomers, each and all, had a pair of wings covered with green feathers growing from their shoulders, and long, purple tails."

"How many of these beings were there, father?"

"Exactly three million and forty-one male adults and three female adults. These creatures first appeared on Earth on the island of Sardinia. In five weeks' time they were the masters of the entire globe."

"Didn't the Earthlings fight back, papa?"

"The humans warred against the invaders, using bullets, ordinary bombs, super-atom bombs, and gases."

"What were those things like, father?"

"Oh, they passed out of existence long ago. 'Ammunition' they were called. The humans fought each other with such things."

"And not with ideas, like we do now, father?"

"No, with guns, just as I told you. But the invaders were immune to the ammunition."

"What does 'immune' mean?"

"Proof against harm. Then the humans tried germs and bacteria against the Star beings."

"What were those things?"

"Tiny, tiny bugs that the humans tried to inject into the bodies of the invaders to make them sicken and die. But the bugs had no effect at all on the Star beings."

"Go on, papa. These beings overran all Earth. Go on from there."

"You must know, these newcomers were much more intelligent than the Earthlings. In fact, the invaders were the greatest mathematicians in the System."

"What's the System? And what does 'mathematician' mean?"

"The Milky Way. A mathematician is one who is good at figuring, weighing, measuring, clever with numbers."

"Then, father, the invaders killed off all the Earthlings?"

"Not all. They killed many, but many others were enslaved. Just as the humans had used horses and cattle, the newcomers so used the humans. They made workers out of some, and others they killed for food."

"Papa, what sort of language did these Star beings talk?"

"A very simple language, but the humans were never able to master it. So, the invaders, being so much smarter, mastered all the languages of the globe."

"What did the Earthlings call the invaders, father?"

" 'An-vils.' Half angels, half devils."

"Then papa, everything was peaceful on Earth after the An-vils enslaved the humans?"

"For a little while. Then, some of the most daring of the humans, led by a man named Knowall, escaped into Greenland. This Knowall was a psychiatrist, the foremost on Earth."

"What's a psychiatrist?"

66

"A dealer in ideas."

"Then, he was very rich?"

"He'd been the richest human on Earth. After some deep thought, Knowall figured a way to rid the earth of the An-vils."

"How papa?"

"He developed a method, called the Knowall-Hughes technique, of imbuing these An-vils with human feelings."

"What does 'imbuing' mean?"

"He filled them full of and made them aware of."

Zenia interrupted, "Aren't you talking a bit above the child's understanding, Drake?"

"No, Mama," said Zoe. "I understand what papa explained. Now, don't interrupt."

"So," continued Drake, "Knowall filled the An-vils with human feelings such as love, hate, ambition, jealousy, envy, despair, hope, fear, shame, and so on. Very soon the An-vils were acting like humans, and in ten days terrible civil wars wiped out two-thirds of the An-vil population."

"Then papa, the An-vils finally killed off each other?"

"Almost, until among them a being named Zalibar, full of saintliness and persuasion, preached the brotherhood of all An-vils. The invaders, quickly persuaded, quit their quarrels, and the Earthlings were even more enslaved."

"Oh, papa, weren't Knowall and his followers in Greenland awfully sad the way things had turned out?"

"For a while. Then Knowall came up with the final payoff."

"Is that slang, papa? Payoff?"

"Yes. The ace in the hole that he'd saved, if all else failed."

"I understand, papa. The idea that would beat anything the other side had to offer. What was it, father? What did they have?"

"Knowall imbued the An-vils with nostalgia."

"What is nostalgia?"

"Homesickness."

"Oh, papa, wasn't Knowall smart? That meant, the An-vils were all filled with the desire to fly back to the Star from where they had started."

"Exactly. So, one day, all the An-vils, a huge army, flapping their great green wings, gathered in the Black Hills of North America, and, at a given signal, they all rose up from Earth and all the humans chanted, 'Glory, glory, the day of our freedom!' "

"So then, father, all the An-vils flew away from Earth?"

"Not all. There were two child An-vils, one male and one female, aged two years, who had been born on Earth, and they started off with all the other An-vils and flew up into the sky. But when they reached the upper limits, they stopped, turned tail, and fluttered back to Earth. Their names were Zizzo and Zizza."

"And what happened to Zizzo and Zizza, papa?"

"Well, like all the An-vils, they were great mathematicians. So, they multiplied."

"Oh, papa," laughed Zoe, flapping her wings excitedly, "that was a very nice story!"

Recall

1. The creatures from Sirius were (a) exactly like humans (b) somewhat like humans (c) nothing like humans.
2. The An-vils took over the earth (a) quite quickly (b) after years of fighting (c) only when Zalibar preached brotherhood.
3. Most of the An-vils left Earth because of (a) the Earthlings' weapons (b) hunger (c) homesickness.
4. The Hawkins family turn out to be (a) An-vils (b) angels (c) devils.

Infer

5. The word in the first paragraph that gives a clue as to the story's ending is (a) garden (b) fluttering (c) quit.
6. Perhaps the *most* unusual feature of this story is that (a) it has a trick ending (b) it contains conversation (c) some of the harder words are defined by one of the characters.
7. The author suggests that humans would be better if they (a) mastered the art of flying (b) used more big words (c) fought with ideas, not weapons and ammunition.
8. The author suggests that human feelings and emotions (a) make life worth living (b) are nearly always right and good (c) often lead to trouble.
9. It is reasonable to think that Zoe, the little girl in the story, (a) has a tail (b) can't fly (c) didn't really like the story.
10. "The Mathematicians" could reasonably be called (a) an accurate view of the future (b) a story with absolutely no meaning (c) a story within a story.

Vocabulary Review

On your paper write the word in *italics* that belongs in each blank. Use each word only once.

enslave   *invader*   *persuasion*
hammock   *organ*   *saintliness*

1. Some American Indians consider the white man to be the ——————— of their country.
2. Too often the white man used his gun as a means of —— ————.
3. The white man tried, but he could never ——————— the Indians.

4. In truth, there was little —————— in the white man's treatment of the Indian.
5. The liver is an —————— that continuously purifies the blood.
6. Did you ever try to lie on your stomach in a ——————?

Critical Thinking

1. "The Mathematicians" is unusual in that it consists almost entirely of *dialog,* or conversation. There are hardly any "tags" like *he said* or *she said.* Yet, the reader can follow it easily and is almost never confused. Look back at the story and explain why. Also explain how this unusual way of writing is especially good for this particular story. Consider the last paragraph of the story in your explanation.
2. How does the father define *psychiatrist?* Why does Zoe assume that "he was very rich"? Exactly what does the father mean by "the richest human on Earth"?
3. Why were Zizzo and Zizza immune to the nostalgia? (Look at the story for the definitions of *immune* and *nostalgia* if you wish.)
4. The next to the last paragraph of the story contains a joke that some readers don't get. Can you explain it?
5. Although "The Mathematicians" is a very light, clever story, it does have some serious things to say about human beings. Express one of these things in a sentence.

Mrs. Hinck

Miriam Allen de Ford

"Mrs. Hinck"? What kind of a title is that?

Why would a professional writer like Miriam Allen de Ford choose to call a story "Mrs. Hinck"? The title tells us almost nothing. You won't find hinck in the dictionary, and unless you live in a huge city, you're not likely to find a Hinck in the phone book. Does the word contain some kind of message? Turned around, it spells kcnih—an unpronounceable scramble. Does it stand for something like 'Her intentions none can know"? Probably not; that's too far out.

Yet "Mrs. Hinck" is the perfect title for the story that follows. In a few minutes you'll see why.

Vocabulary Preview

ABROAD (uh BRAWD) overseas; in or to a
foreign country
    • Pam joined the WAACS because she
wanted to travel *abroad.*

AFFECTIONS (uh FEK shuns) feelings of love or
friendship
    • The Steele family all have strong
affections for one another.

PASSPORT (PASS port) an official paper
allowing a citizen of one country to travel
in another
    • You can't go to England without a U.S.
passport.

RECKLESSLY (REK lis lee) carelessly;
dangerously
    • I often speak *recklessly* and regret it
later.

SESSION (SESH un) a meeting or lesson
    • Every Tuesday Hank has a *session*
with his guitar teacher.

VOLUNTARILY (VOL un TER uh lee) of one's
own choice; without being forced
    • Lester cleaned the house *voluntarily* to
surprise his family.

I'D LIKE AN OLDER, MORE SETTLED woman if I could get one—somebody reliable," Gwen said into the telephone. "I've had high school girls and they invite their friends and play the phonograph all hours and keep the children awake. . . . Two, a boy eight and a girl five. . . . Oh, that would be fine. Could she come tomorrow at six?"

Mrs. Hinck arrived promptly on the hour, a comfortable, grandmotherly sort of person. Gav and Ada seemed to take to her at once. Best of all, Dale wouldn't have to drive her home when they got back; she came in her own little two-seater, which she parked outside.

"Give the children their supper as soon as we leave," Gwen instructed her. "It's all ready in the kitchen. Ada's bedtime is eight and Gav can stay up till half-past. He can take care of himself, but you'll have to help Ada a little. And oh, yes, much as we dislike it"—Gwen made a sour little smile and Mrs. Hinck smiled sympathetically—"there's a riproaring program on television that they won't be happy without. It comes on at 7:30."

"Now don't you worry about anything," said Mrs. Hinck. "We're going to get along beautifully."

It was after one when Gwen and Dale got home. The only light was in the living room, where Mrs. Hinck sat quietly knitting something in yellow wool. She had even cleaned up the children's supper dishes. Gwen breathed a sigh of relief, remembering the high school girls.

"It's after midnight, so we owe you an hour overtime," Dale said.

"Nonsense," responded Mrs. Hinck. "I always sit up late anyhow, and I'm just knitting here instead of at home."

73

Gwen and Dale exchanged unbelieving glances.

"Would you have time to come often—say twice a week?" Gwen asked. She didn't want to be more specific till she found out how the kids had liked her. "I'll phone in the morning—what's your number?"

"I'm sorry, but I haven't any phone," said Mrs. Hinck. "Just call the agency—I check with them every day."

She folded the yellow wool into a knitting bag, put on her smart black hat and coat, and drove away.

"Well, kids, what happened to Roaring Roger last night?" Dale inquired at the breakfast table.

Gav and Ada stared at each other blankly.

"Well, for gosh sake!" Gav exploded. "We forgot all about him! Mrs. Hinck was telling us a story."

"Do you like her?"

"She's swell," they said together.

It was grand, being able to get out again together. Gwen was a devoted mother, but you can't help being young and wanting a little fun sometimes. On Mrs. Hinck's second evening, they arranged for Wednesdays and Saturdays, regularly.

"And maybe an extra evening once in a while, if you're not too busy," Gwen said recklessly.

"Any time—just let the agency know. To tell the truth, this is all the baby-sitting I'm doing right now. But I'd love to come here whenever you say. I like children, and I get so lonesome for my own little granddaughter. This is a sweater for her that I'm knitting.

"How old is she?" Gwen asked.

"Just about a year older than your Ada. I miss her a lot."

"Isn't she here in the city?"

"Oh, no, my daughter lives abroad. She married a for-eigner: Illinck is his name. I was with them for a while, but I don't know when I'll go back. I just get the urge to wander in

74

my old age, and decided to travel, and now I seem to have settled down here. I do miss Mary, though—and my daughter too, of course. I guess Mary misses me too. She's an only child, and there are no other children around. I wish she had your little boy and girl to play with. They're lovely youngsters."

"We think so," Dale grinned. "Thanks a lot, by the way, for avoiding that blood-and-thunder TV program. How did you do it?"

"Oh, I just tell them stories," Mrs. Hinck said vaguely. "I guess they just get interested and forget the television. I did the same way with Mary when I was there. They don't have television, but it was the same thing with radio."

"Illinck," Dale remarked after Mrs. Hinck had left. "That's a funny name—wonder what nationality he is?"

"I can't imagine. Don't let's ask any questions. Dale, there might be some family trouble. I noticed she didn't want to say much. And we don't want to offend her and lose her— we're too lucky."

"*I'm* the one that's lucky," Dale retorted, "getting a chance again to go places with my best girl."

Nevertheless, Gwen couldn't avoid a tiny bit of jealousy when Gav and Ada began watching from the front window for Mrs. Hinck, and rushing to the door to greet her with hugs.

"Don't be a goof," she scolded herself. "She isn't stealing your kids' affections—they're as fond of us as ever. They just needed a grandmother, and she needed some grandchildren."

On summer evenings when it was still light after dinner and they weren't going anywhere, Dale would cut the grass or water the front garden. That was the signal for Gav and Ada to perch on the bottom step of the porch and draw him into the conversation.

"Daddy, why don't I have a grandmother?" That was Ada.

"You have—you've got two of them, and two grandfathers too, only they live way off at the other end of the country. They send you Christmas and birthday presents—don't you remember? Maybe some day one of them will visit us."

"Whenever Mrs. Hinck goes to visit her granddaughter, she takes her simply wonderful toys," said Ada, in a wistful voice.

"Well, if one of your grandmothers comes to see you, she'll bring you toys, too."

"Not like Mrs. Hinck," Ada said stubbornly. "Mrs. Hinck brings Mary toys like nobody else in the world has—she told us so."

"Pig," remarked Gav. "Hey, daddy, can I hold the hose for a while now, huh?"

"I'm getting a little tired of Mrs. Hinck's granddaughter," Dale commented later to Gwen. "She must be the worst spoiled brat in creation."

"She does seem kind of hung up on the subject, doesn't she? But she's lonely, I guess, poor old thing."

"Just so she doesn't give our kids ideas. Toys like none in the whole word—gosh!"

Another evening, and another gardening session.

"When Mrs. Hinck visits her granddaughter," said Gav, "she doesn't use a train or a bus or a ship or a plane to get there."

"That's nice. What does she do—walk and swim?"

"No, she just *goes*."

Curiosity got the better of Dale.

"She ever tell you the name of the country where her granddaughter lives?"

"Sure. It's called America, just like this one."

"America, eh? And what language do they speak there?"

76

"Why, English, just like us, of course."

Dale felt ashamed of his prying. Mrs. Hinck obviously had forestalled any possible questions on his or Gwen's part. He changed the subject.

"How's your granddaughter's sweater coming along?" Gwen asked Mrs. Hinck the next time she came.

"Almost done. I'm going to make a cap to match. It's for her seventh birthday. Some time this fall I might just pop over and visit there—I do miss Mary so much. How I wish I could take your two along! It would be wonderful for Mary."

"Yes, it's too bad it's so far away," Gwen answered absentmindedly. Her heart sank. There would never be another Mrs. Hinck, and she and Dale had been having such good times together. "But you'd be back, wouldn't you?" she asked hopefully.

"Oh, I think so, unless—well, anyways, we needn't think about it yet."

That was in August. On Saturday night in the first week of October Dale and Gwen went to a party. They hated to be the first ones to break it up. It was after three when they drove up to their door.

"I feel guilty, keeping that poor old lady up so late," Gwen murmured.

"She's gone to sleep, I guess," Dale told her. "There's no light in the living room."

Gwen let out a startled cry.

"Dale!" she gasped. "Look—her car isn't here. She *couldn't* have gone home and left the children alone in the house—not Mrs. Hinck!"

They raced in. There was no one in the living room or anywhere else on the first floor. Together they ran upstairs, the same sudden terror in their hearts.

The two little bedrooms were dark, and the beds were empty. They had not been slept in.

77

Gwen's knees failed her. Dale dashed to the phone to call the police.

"Gwen," he shouted back from the hall, "what's the license number of Mrs. Hinck's car? I never noticed."

"I never did either," Gwen moaned.

It was almost dawn—with Gwen in tears and Dale walking the floor—before the police called back. They'd found the license number at last, from the records, and they'd sent a man to the address Mrs. Hinck had given as hers. It was an all-night parking lot.

The night man there knew Mrs. Hinck by sight, but he hadn't seen her since he came on duty at eight. She kept her car there all the time, paying by the month, that was all he knew.

The whole long day was a nightmare. Neither of them had slept, and they kept going on black coffee, for they couldn't eat. A detective had appeared early in the morning and looked at the children's rooms. Nothing of theirs or of their parents' was missing, and there were no signs of struggle, or any evidence that a disturber had been there.

"They were kidnapped, all right," the detective concluded. "But they must have gone voluntarily."

What does "voluntarily" mean, when it is applied to children of five and eight?

Dale told him about the daughter who had married a foreigner named Illinck and lived abroad.

"Never heard of such a name," said the detective. "That all you know about him? We'll send out a general alarm right away, of course, but I don't see how she could leave the country without a passport." He took out his notebook. "Now give me a full description of the little girl and boy. And this Mrs. Hinck—what does she look like?"

"About five feet five, rather plump, nicely curled white hair, glasses in a gold frame."

It sounded like the description of half the grandmothers in the world.

"Well, that helps a lot," said the detective with false encouragement. "No ransom note, I suppose, or anything like that?"

"No, nothing at all."

"And there won't be, I'm sure of that," Dale put in. "This isn't a kidnapping for money; the old lady seemed to be very well off. It's more like—well, the way I figure it out, she grew fond of our kids and that's why she took them."

"We get plenty of cases like that, though it's usually younger women. By the way, we've checked with the manager of the agency you got her from. They don't know a thing about her. She just came in there and signed up one day. They sent her out half a dozen times but she didn't seem to like the people and wouldn't go to any of them again, till they sent her to you. And the only address she gave was what turned out to be that parking lot."

"I'm absolutely positive," Gwen insisted, "that she's gone to her daughter and granddaughter, and taken Gav and Ada with her. She told me she might make a visit to them this fall, and she said something, months ago, about wishing she could take our two along with her. I thought she was just talking. And of course I expected she'd tell us ahead of time when she planned to leave."

"Neither did you think she'd snatch your children when she went, naturally. Well, folks, don't lose heart. I have kids of my own, and I know how you feel. But we're on the job, and we'll stay on it. We ought to have results very soon. From what you've told me, there isn't a chance she'd do any harm to them. And if she makes any attempt to take them out of the country—"

"Oh, the secret journey! I just remembered. Gav said to me only yesterday, 'Mrs. Hinck says some day she'll take us on a secret journey to a strange place.' I just laughed—I never even thought—"

"The only strange place she's going to see is the inside of a jail," the detective said.

But day passed into night again, and still there was no word of progress. They had tried again to eat but the food choked them. Finally, they did drop asleep for an hour or two in the late afternoon, until the phone shocked them awake. But it was only the detective, to say that Mrs. Hinck's car had been found parked in the driveway of a vacant house at the other end of the city.

Husband and wife stood together at the front window where Gav and Ada had stood so often watching for Mrs. Hinck. They had stood there for a long time, not even bothering to turn on the lights as night came on. Dale held Gwen close to him, and once in a while she wept quietly.

"Look, darling," he said at last gently. "Are you thinking what I'm thinking?"

Gwen lifted a wet face and nodded dumbly. Her lips trembled.

"I felt you were. Looking out here reminded me of things the kids used to talk about to me while I gardened.

"Gwen, you never studied any foreign languages: I did. *Hinc* means *on this side* in Latin, and *illinc* means *from that side.*"

Gwen found a shaky voice.

"And the thing you told me, that Gav said—when Mrs. Hinck goes to visit her granddaughter—"

"She doesn't take a train or a bus or a ship or a plane—she just *goes.* Yes, that too."

"Oh, Dale! there were so many hints we never even noticed. That country's America, too, and the language they speak is English."

"We thought that was funny, or just to keep us from

80

snooping. We'd better face it, Gwen. If we're right, the police can't ever get them back to us. And Mrs. Hinck won't need any passport where she's taken them."

She started to sob again. Dale held her tightly, his own face twisted.

" 'I wish she had your little boy and girl to play with'!" he quoted bitterly.

"The toys!" Gwen whispered. "The toys that are simply wonderful, that aren't like any others in the world—"

Recall

1. One reason Mrs. Hinck first comes to look after the children is that (a) Gwen, the mother, is not satisfied with high school girls (b) Mrs. Hinck is much cheaper (c) Mrs. Hinck is the only person Gwen can find in an emergency.
2. Dale, the father, is very pleased when he first sees Mrs. Hinck's (a) stack of books for the children (b) knitting (c) car.
3. The first evening the children spend with Mrs. Hinck, they (a) go to their rooms and read (b) watch TV (c) listen to her stories.
4. Mrs. Hinck explains to Gwen and Dale that she baby-sits mainly because she (a) needs the money badly (b) likes children (c) has no TV set at home.
5. The man with the strange name of Illinck is Mrs. Hinck's (a) first husband (b) son-in-law (c) cousin.
6. Mrs. Hinck says she's sorry that her granddaughter Mary has (a) only one parent (b) no TV (c) no other children to play with.

7. Gwen and Dale decide not to question Mrs. Hinck too closely because (a) she never answers questions (b) they have absolutely no interest in her personal life (c) they don't want to offend and lose her.

8. When they find the children gone from the house, Gwen and Dale are at first (a) totally surprised (b) sure that Mrs. Hinck took them away for some good reason (c) sure that their suspicions were correct after all.

9. The address Mrs. Hinck had given them turns out to be a (a) police station (b) parking lot (c) vacant house.

10. Right after talking to the detective, the parents believe that Mrs. Hinck has stolen the children to (a) hold them for ransom (b) torture them (c) visit her daughter and granddaughter.

11. It later turns out that Mrs. Hinck has stolen the children to (a) hold them for ransom (b) torture them (c) visit her daughter and granddaughter.

12. Toward the end of the story, proof of what has really happened seems to come from (a) the detective's investigation (b) the Latin meanings of two words (c) Mrs. Hinck's confession.

Infer

13. The "agency" mentioned several times in the story helps people find (a) lost children (b) love and friendship (c) jobs.

14. Gwen and Dale can accurately be described as (a) concerned parents (b) religious persons (c) stay-at-homes.

15. One of several important clues concerning Mrs. Hinck is (a) "I'm the one that's lucky," Dale retorted. (b) "Hey, daddy, can I hold the hose for a while now, huh?" (c) "It's called America, just like this one."

16. The *first* bad feeling that the mother has about Mrs. Hinck's relationship with the children is (a) jealousy (b) rage (c) terror.
17. Mrs. Hinck can best be described as being (a) greedy (b) excitable (c) unusual.
18. After listening to the description of Mrs. Hinck, the detective says, "Well, that helps a lot." With these words, he (a) hints that he understands the truth of what has happened (b) says what he really means (c) says the opposite of what he really means.
19. Several clues in the story indicate that Mrs. Hinck has taken the children to (a) a Latin country (b) somewhere very much like America (c) the other side of the world.
20. It is reasonable to suppose that Gwen and Dale are afraid they will (a) never see their children again (b) have to pay a ransom to Mrs. Hinck (c) be arrested by the police.

Vocabulary Review

Write on your paper the term in *italics* that belongs in each blank. Use each term only once.

abroad　　　*passport*　　　*session*
affections　　*recklessly*　　*voluntarily*

1. Armand was late for his ——————— with the guidance counselor.
2. If you're jealous, you think you've lost someone's ——— ———.
3. It's better to do your homework ——————— than it is to do it ———————.
4. Only in a few special cases can American citizens travel ———————without a ———————.

Critical Thinking

1. Did you guess the ending of the story before it happened? If so, look back and find the two clues that helped you the most. If not, look back for two clues that might have helped.

2. Explain this sentence on page 78: "What does 'voluntarily' mean, when it is applied to children of five and eight?"

3. Mrs. Hinck had not liked any of the other families the agency had sent her to. Explain the best possible reason.

4. In the language of science fiction, visitors from outer space are called *aliens*. Both the last story, "The Mathematicians," and "Mrs. Hinck" are about aliens. In what ways are the aliens in these two stories different? In what ways are they similar?

5. Read the following paragraphs carefully. When you finish, explain what they have to do with "Mrs. Hinck."

"Some scientists believe in an *unlimited universe*. In other words, the universe—planets, stars, all there is—has no end but just goes outward and outward forever. If you could travel to the farthest star, you'd find beyond it another "farthest star," because the universe has no limits.

"But if the universe has no limits in space, there are also no limits to what can happen in the universe. In fact, without limits, *everything* that might possibly happen *is* happening somewhere. This means that somewhere there exists another world like ours, another country like the United States, and perhaps even another person just like you."

The Flatwoods Monster

Frank Edwards

Science fiction or scientific fact? Sometimes it's hard to tell the difference. At times fiction leads to fact. Electric thinking machines, metal warships, rockets to other planets, lie detectors, long-distance submarines, parachutes—all existed in the pages of sci-fi before they existed in fact. At other times fact seems more like fiction. Things happen that most people simply cannot believe. So it is with the tale that follows. It is told as a true story. The people involved in it believed that it really happened. You'll have to make up your own mind about what occurred in the little West Virginia town of Flatwoods a few years ago.

Vocabulary Preview

AROMA (uh ROE muh) a smell or odor
> • The *aroma* of frying bacon filled the house.

BRISTLE (BRIS l) to have the bristles, or short hairs, stand on end, as in the case of an angry or frightened animal
> • The dog *bristled* and then barked at the strange old woman.

HYSTERICAL (his STER uh kul) terribly excited; totally out of control
> • Mr. Hepprich became *hysterical* when he saw the car hit his child.

PULSATE (PUHL sate) to increase and decrease with a regular rhythm, like the pulse
> • The police car had a *pulsating* red light on its top.

PUNGENT (PUN junt) having a sharp, strong smell
> • The air was *pungent* with the smell of new paint.

SKEPTICAL (SKEP tih kuhl) doubtful; disbelieving
> • Until *I* see a flying saucer, I'm going to be *skeptical* about them!

Those who saw the thing were terri-
fied. Those who investigated were certain that it had been
there. But what it was and where it came from remain unan-
swered questions. We are left with the mystery of the Flatwoods monster.

It was just getting dark on that warm September evening. The five youngsters stopped their play to watch the
strange sight overhead. Outlined against the sky over the
nearby mountains was a round, flat object. It was leaving
behind it little streams of sparks. It wobbled a bit, moved on
slowly and dropped down toward the mountaintop. It settled
among the trees.

Whatever it was, it did not look like any plane the youngsters had ever seen. They realized that this was some sort of
emergency. They scattered to their homes to report. Eddie
May, 13, and his brother Fred, 12, ran to the nearby house
where their mother operated a beauty parlor in the little West
Virginia community of 300 people.

The boys told their mother excitedly that they and their
friends had seen a plane or a flying saucer land on the hill
that towered above the town.

Mrs. May was skeptical, of course. But her doubts disappeared when she stepped outside to see for herself. There,
glowing dimly several hundred yards away near the top of
the hill, was a slowly pulsating red light. Something was on
the ground there, just as the children had said . . . but what
was it? Mrs. May sent the boys running to the nearby home
of Gene Lemon, 17, a member of the National Guard.

Armed only with a flashlight, Lemon led the party up the
hill. In addition to Mrs. May and her two sons, the group

also included 14-year-old Neil Nunley, and a pair of ten-year-olds who had also seen the object land, Ronnie Shaver and Tommy Hyer.

The experience they had in the minutes that followed put the little community of Flatwoods on the front pages of the world's newspapers.

Lemon and the Nunley boy were about fifty feet ahead of the rest of the party as they hurried up the brush-covered hillside.

They noticed a light mist which drifted before them. As they got closer they smelled a pungent, disagreeable odor about it. Near the top of the hill the unpleasant odor was strongest. They spotted a glowing red object which pulsated slowly . . . like a faintly glowing mass of red coals, they said. For the moment they forgot about the pungent aroma that swirled about them. Lemon and Nunley reached an old gateway from which they could see the red object clearly . . . a thing about 25 feet across and perhaps six feet high. . . . Should they approach it? As they paused, Mrs. May and the other boys joined them.

The attention of the entire group was directed to this strange glowing thing on the ground about seventy-five feet away. And for a moment, none of the group noticed the other object, hardly twenty feet away, among the bushes to their right.

The dog that had gone with the party growled and bristled, and the entire group turned to see what was wrong. Gene Lemon flashed his light among the bushes. Mrs. May screamed.

Whatever it was, it was alive . . . and it was a giant. The flashlight showed the head and shoulders of a creature slightly less than ten feet tall. It appeared to be wearing a helmet of some sort above a dark blue-green or greenish-gray body which reflected the flashlight beam.

88

The most frightening part of the scene was the thing's face . . . almost round and blood red . . . with two greenish-orange eyes which glowed in the flashlight beams as do the eyes of certain fish and some wild animals. But this was neither fish nor wild animal.

The thing moved. The lower part of its body was hidden by the brush and weeds . . . but all agreed that it didn't walk . . . it seemed to slide its feet, if it had any. There was a hissing sound, and a powerful sickening odor filled the air.

Lemon's dog ran away. Lemon dropped his flashlight. The entire party of seven panicked and raced pell-mell down the hillside. Once safely away from the scene of their terrifying experience, they phoned the Sheriff at nearby Sutton, West Virginia. He and a deputy were miles away on another call to check on a report that a plane had crashed . . . possibly the same object that had been seen at Flatwoods. Someone notified Lee Stewart, Jr., editor of the Braxton newspaper. . . . He reached Flatwoods in about thirty minutes and found Mrs. May hysterical . . . the boys in a state of shock.

Finally Gene Lemon led another armed party back to the hilltop. The strange, sickening odor was still there . . . but the monster and the huge pulsating red object were gone.

Not without a trace, however. For in the soil where the horrible red object had stood, the searching party found unexplained skid marks . . . which may have been the only earthly sign of the Flatwoods monster.

Recall

1. The strange object was first seen in the sky by (a) Mrs. May (b) Gene Lemon (c) five youngsters.

2. The first thing to interest the group of investigators was (a) a blue light (b) a bad smell (c) a hissing sound.
3. The flying saucer was (a) cigar shaped (b) about 25 feet wide (c) filled with little round windows.
4. The odd-looking creature standing nearby was first noticed by (a) the ten-year-olds (b) Gene Lemon (c) the dog.
5. The first outsider to reach the scene of the mystery was a (a) sheriff (b) sheriff's deputy (c) newspaper editor.

Infer

6. Mrs. May's reason for sending for Lemon was probably that (a) Lemon had a gun (b) Lemon investigates reports of flying saucers (c) she was frightened.
7. The author's reason for NOT calling the strange creature a "man" was probably that (a) the thing was too inhuman (b) the word "man" would suggest a joker dressed in a costume (c) he thought the creature was female rather than male.
8. The fact that the group ran away in terror indicates that (a) they were foolish people who were too easily frightened (b) the creature was truly frightening (c) the "monster" must have been created by joker.
9. The skid marks (a) prove that the people were mistaken (b) indicate that a flying saucer *may* have landed (c) are *not* an important part of the story.
10. The author of the selection seems (a) to believe that Mrs. May, Lemon, and the others told the truth as they saw it (b) doubtful that the events really occurred (c) to have made up the story himself.

90

Vocabulary Review

Write on your paper the word in *italics* that belongs in each blank. Use each word only once.

bristle *pulsate* *skeptical*
hysterical *pungent*

1. A ———————— aroma is the same thing as a sharp smell.
2. To ———————— is the same thing as to have your hair "stand on end."
3. If you look closely at the inside of your wrist, you may see your blood ————————.
4. To doubt something is to be ————————.
5. When crowds of people become ———————— they can easily panic in confusion.

Critical Thinking

1. One way of determining the truth of this story is to ask if the actions of the people involved seem natural. For instance, do you believe that a group of children who really thought they had seen a flying saucer land would have the courage to go and investigate? Would Mrs. May have gone? What about other actions in the story? Explain your thinking.
2. One possible explanation of the story is that the seven people who "investigated" made up the whole story to get their names in the paper. After all, the skid marks and the smell were the only "proof" offered to others. In your opinion, how likely is this explanation to be the right one?
3. Another possible explanation is that the seven investigators were fooled by other people who had created a compli-

cated joke. First describe how the flying saucer and the creature might have been made to appear. Then tell how likely
you believe this explanation to be.

4. Still another possible explanation, of course, is that the
strange events did, in fact, really happen. How likely is this
explanation? Is there any way to prove that the events did *not*
really occur? Why or why not?

The Mansion of Forgetfulness

Don Mark Lemon

As we know, there's nothing new about science fiction. Your great-great-grandfather may never have heard of radios, TV sets, supermarkets, or jet planes. But chances are he did read sci-fi. The newsstands of his day were crowded with magazines like The Owl, The All-Story Magazine, *and* The Black Cat, *all of which published stories that today we'd call sci-fi. Many of these old stories deserve to be better known. Here, for instance, is a weird tale that first appeared in the April 1907 issue of* The Black Cat. *It was recently rediscovered and republished by a sci-fi expert named Sam Moskowitz. Let's give Mr. Moscowitz credit for finding a great story about forgetfulness that should never be forgotten.*

Vocabulary Preview

FREE WILL (FREE WILL) free choice; the
power to choose freely
   • Aunt Margaret chose of her own *free
   will* to become a nun.

IDENTITY (i DEN tih tee) a person's name;
those things that make a person known to
others
   • Dressed in her ghost costume, little
   Bonnie kept her *identity* a secret.

PILGRIM (PILL grum) a traveler, usually
moving toward some religious goal
   • The *pilgrims* finally reached the Holy
   Land.

RECOGNITION (REK ug NISH un) the act of
recognizing a person or thing
   • Lying in the hospital bed, Dad showed
   no signs of *recognition* when I entered the
   room.

VEIL (VAIL) a piece of cloth worn in front of
the face
   • In some countries women wear *veils*
   over their faces.

WITHER (WITH ur) to dry up, shrink, and
fade
   • The hot sun *withered* the wild flowers
   Dean had picked along the road.

FOUR MONTHS HAD PASSED SINCE THE SALT waves of the sea had laid at his feet the cold form of his love. And now a few people who knew him well learned that Herbert Munson was the owner of an amazing discovery. He had discovered a Purple Ray that would destroy certain cells of memory in the human brain. Certain memories could now be blotted out without danger to the rest of the brain. This story was followed by the still more amazing report that Munson had built a Mansion of Forgetfulness. To this Mansion anyone who wanted to free his or her mind of a hopeless memory might go, and in one brief hour, *forget.*

And, sure enough, here they came—those who had loved not wisely but too well, those who loved deeply but hopelessly, those who loved the Dead and could stand their sadness no longer. The Purple Ray removed their memories. They went forth from the Mansion of Forgetfulness smiling and fancy free.

Yet the very man who showed others how to forget would not himself forget. It was terrible to know that she was dead. He would never see her face again, but he could not bring himself to forget her. Try as he would, he could not drag himself from his memories. He knew that the outside world was full of wonderful things. That other women, perhaps as lovely as she, were waiting there to love and be loved. No! Let others forget, he would not! Not that he lived in hope, for had he not kissed the salt foam from her dead face? But that memory was all that remained of a Love who was no more.

He watched them come and go—watched the many, ah, too many, pilgrims arrive with sad, love-haunted faces, but depart looking happy and free of care. And at times he feared that what he was doing was somehow not right. There seemed something wrong in this sudden transformation of

95

grief into gladness, this quick destruction of all sorrow. Yet the pilgrims had chosen of their own free will to forget their hopeless loves. They could now return to where they came from and love again, more wisely if less deeply.

Some came, wanting to blot out other memories than that of a hopeless love—memories of sin and crime—but the Purple Ray would not work for such an evil purpose, and they left, deeply disappointed.

It was in winter. The snow fell softly upon the walls and roofs of the beautiful stone building. It piled itself in drifts of diamonds against the stained glass windows. A lady came alone across the valleys and entered the wide doorway of the Mansion of Forgetfulness. She was slim, young, and obviously very sad. A heavy veil hid her face from the world.

Something in her manner—perhaps the way she paused at the door—made the owner speak to her.

"Kind friend," he said, "is it not better to remember what you now want to forget?" As he spoke he drew closer about his face the hood he wore to hide his identity from people who were too curious.

A sigh was the only answer, as the pilgrim leaned tiredly against the door. Then came the low spoken words:

"Perhaps I may only half forget. I would like to remember, yet not remember so well."

"No, you will completely forget. The Purple Ray is forgetfulness itself."

"Ah, well, it is better to kill these painful memories than to break my heart!"

"Then, if it must be so, enter and forget."

"Show me the way and let me go quickly," was the request of the veiled lady. "I have come far, and the worst is only a few steps farther on."

"Come, then!" and the owner led the way to the room of the Purple Ray.

An hour passed, and then the door was opened and the

veiled visitor came forth and descended the broad stairway. She moved quickly and lightly, and at the foot of the stairs she laughed as she again met the owner.

"Have you forgotten?" he asked.

"Forgotten! I know that I have forgotten something, or why am I here? But I do not know what I have forgotten."

"So they all say!"

A glow of rosy light shined down from a slender window overhead. It formed a halo over the pilgrim. She looked like a saint.

"How beautiful everything is!" she exclaimed. "Why do I wear this veil? I will wear it no longer!"

So saying, she loosened it, uncovering a face young and blindingly beautiful. The man shrank back as if struck by lightning.

"My God, it is her spirit!" he gasped.

"No, no!" protested the visitor. "I am not a spirit, and I fear I am too, too human."

"You are Morella!" whispered the man, staring before him like a person trying to see through total darkness.

"Yes, Morella is my name. Who are you that you ask?"

"Morella! I thought you were dead! I kissed you for dead and then the waves swept me away and I saw you no more."

"Some fishermen once found me on a sandy beach, where they said I had fainted. Who are you?"

The man drew back his hood. "Look!" There was no light of recognition in the other's eyes. "My God! The Ray has blotted out all memory!"

"Please tell me what you mean, and let me go," said the woman.

A groan was the only reply, and the man hid his face in his hands.

"You seem to know what I have forgotten," said the woman. "Has it anything to do with you?"

"Oh Morella, it would be better to think you dead than to

know that you have forgotten! Do you not remember that we were engaged? See, you have the ring upon your hand! Does it not bring back one memory of other days?"

The girl gazed blankly at the ring on her hand, and shook her head.

"Has the Ray blotted out every good memory! Have you returned to life only to forget! Try to think! Do you not remember that day in Naples when we swore eternal love for one another?"

"I remember no engagement." A deep look of pity came into the speaker's eyes when she saw the pain her words had caused. "If your memories are so sad, why do you not also forget?"

"My love!" he groaned, "you are making the world darker to me than to dying eyes! *You* ask me to forget! *You!*"

"You forget that I have forgotten."

The man groaned in complete despair.

As she turned to go he stopped her by a gentle touch. *"Wait here while I, too, go and kill that memory!"*

He dragged himself up the broad stairway, looking back once when he had reached the top. Then he turned and staggered toward the room of the Purple Ray.

Recall

1. At the beginning of the story, Herbert Munson was quite sure that Morella had (a) drowned (b) been saved by some fishermen (c) invented the Purple Ray.

2. The Purple Ray worked by (a) changing brain cells to a purple color (b) increasing the number of brain cells that produced happy feelings (c) destroying certain brain cells.

3. The Purple Ray would not work for (a) lovers (b) criminals (c) young persons.

4. When Munson first met Morella at the door of the Mansion (a) she recognized him but he didn't recognize her (b) he recognized her but she didn't recognize him (c) neither recognized the other.

5. Munson learned the truth of what had happened when (a) Morella saw his face and fainted (b) he pulled back his hood (c) Morella loosened her veil.

6. Munson's solution to his problem was to (a) make Morella's memory whole again (b) kill his own memories (c) destroy the Purple Ray machine.

Infer

7. No date is given in the story; but it seems to be happening in the (a) past (b) present (c) future.

8. Herbert Munson had never used the Purple Ray on himself, probably because (a) he felt that even a sad memory of Morella was better than no memory of her at all (b) he thought it absolutely wrong for anyone to use the Purple Ray (c) he expected to meet Morella again.

9. The words *pilgrim, halo,* and *saint* suggest that (a) Morella had given her life to religious service (b) the story takes place in Europe (c) to Munson, there was something holy about Morella and their love.

10. Of the following, which is most likely? (a) Herbert Munson will kill himself (b) The Mansion of Forgetfulness will explode (c) Munson and Morella will go their separate ways.

Vocabulary Review

1. The people who landed at Plymouth Rock in 1620 were called *Pilgrims* because (a) of the way they dressed (b) they were traveling for a religious purpose (c) they were grim people.

2. A person who doesn't believe in *free will* thinks that (a) freedom is everybody's job (b) most adults have freely chosen their careers (c) most of our actions are forced upon us.
3. A piece of clothing to cover the head and shoulders is a (a) tight (b) veil (c) doublet.
4. If your *identity* is a secret, no one knows (a) who you really are (b) whether you're alive or dead (c) where you are at any given time.
5. A teacher who shows you little *recognition* would probably not (a) mark your tests fairly (b) call on you much in class (c) explain things clearly.
6. The word *withered* used to describe a person would probably refer mainly to the person's (a) generosity (b) speech (c) skin.

Critical Thinking

1. Why did Herbert Munson sometimes see something wrong in the Purple Ray? Do you agree with him? Explain.
2. Why might it be better for unhappy lovers to forget certain things than for criminals to forget certain past actions?
3. The Purple Ray, of course, is an impossibility. But what about the rest of the story? Is there anything else that probably would not happen? Think particularly about the reasons the characters act as they do.
4. Look up *irony* in the dictionary. How does the irony in "The Mansion of Forgetfulness" make it a better story?
5. Think of one troublesome memory that you think it would be good for you to forget. What is this memory? Why would forgetting it do you more good than harm? Think of something you could discuss with the class rather than something very personal.

Who's Cribbing?

Jack Lewis

*What would you do? You've written a good
story for English and passed it in to your teacher.
When you get the story back, the teacher accuses
you of having copied it. He is absolutely certain
that exactly the same story was handed in by
another student several years before. Yet you are
absolutely certain that every word in your story is
original. What would you do?*

*If you're as clever as Jack Lewis, you might try
using the odd experience as the idea for another
story. "Who's Cribbing?" was written back in
1952 and is well on its way to becoming a classic.
Sci-fi fans just won't let it die. Get set for a flip-
flop.*

Vocabulary Preview

ACCUSATION (AK yu ZAY shun) a charge of
doing something bad
   • The teacher's *accusation* that Eileen
   had cheated made her mad.

BARRIER (BARE ee ur) something that blocks
the way or keeps people from passing
   • Only in sci-fi stories can people pass
   through *barriers* of time and space.

CRIBBING (KRIB ing) copying to cheat or fool
others
   • The teacher accused Eileen of *cribbing*
   during the test.

MANUSCRIPT (MAN yu skript) a story or
article in handwritten or typed form
   ⌣ An editor's job is to prepare
   manuscripts for printing.

OCCURRENCE (uh KUR uns) a happening;
anything that occurs
   • What's the strangest *occurrence* in your
   life?

PLAGIARISM (PLAY ju riz um) passing off the
writings of another person as one's own
   • Most schools have strict penalties
   against *plagiarism.*

April 2, 1952

Mr. Jack Lewis
90-26 219 St.
Queens Village, N.Y.

Dear Mr. Lewis:

We are returning your manuscript "The Ninth Dimension." At first glance, I had figured it a story well worthy of publishing. Why wouldn't I? So did the editors of *Cosmic Tales* back in 1934 when the story was first published.

As you no doubt know, it was the great Todd Thromberry who wrote the story you tried to pass off on us as an original. Let me give you a word of warning concerning the penalties resulting from plagiarism.

It's not worth it. Believe me.

Sincerely,
Doyle P. Gates
Science Fiction Editor
Deep Space Magazine

April 5, 1952

Mr. Doyle P. Gates, Editor
Deep Space Magazine
New York, N.Y.

Dear Mr. Gates:

I do not know, nor am I aware of the existence of any Todd Thromberry. The story you sent back was submitted in good faith, and I dislike the suggestion that I plagiarized it.

"The Ninth Dimension" was written by me not more than a month ago, and if there is any similarity between it

103

and the story written by this Thromberry person, it is purely accidental.

However, it has set me thinking. Some time ago, I submitted another story to *Stardust Scientification* and received a penciled note stating that the story was, "too thromber-rish."

Who in the hell is Todd Thromberry? I don't remember reading anything written by him in the ten years I've been interested in science fiction.

Sincerely,
Jack Lewis

April 11, 1952

Mr. Jack Lewis
90-26 219 St.
Queens Village, N.Y.

Dear Mr. Lewis:

This is a reply to your letter of April 5.

While the editors of this magazine are not in the habit of making open accusations and are well aware of the fact in the writing business there will always be some overlapping of plot ideas, it is very hard for us to believe that you are not familiar with the stories of Todd Thromberry.

While Mr. Thromberry is no longer among us, his stories, like so many other writers', only became widely recognized after his death in 1941. Perhaps it was his work in the field of electricity that supplied him with the bottomless pit of new ideas so obvious in all his works. Nevertheless, even at this stage of science fiction's development it is clear that he had a style that many of our so-called modern writers might do well to copy. By "copy," I do not mean rewrite word for word one or more of his stories, as you have done. For while you state this has been accidental surely you must realize that the chance of this actually happening is about a million times as great as the occurrence of four royal flushes on one deal at the poker table.

Sorry, but we're not that stupid.

Sincerely yours,
Doyle P. Gates
Science Fiction Editor
Deep Space Magazine

April 14, 1952

Mr. Doyle P. Gates, Editor
Deep Space Magazine
New York, N.Y.

Sir:

Your accusations are typical of the rag you publish. Please cancel my subscription immediately.

Sincerely,
Jack Lewis

April 14, 1952

Science Fiction Society
144 Front Street
Chicago, Ill.

Gentlemen:

I am interested in reading some of the stories of the late Todd Thromberry.

I would like to get some of the magazines that feature his stories.

Respectfully,
Jack Lewis
105

April 22, 1952

Mr. Jack Lewis
90-26 219 St.
Queens Village, N.Y.

Dear Mr. Lewis:

So would we. All I can suggest is that you contact the magazines if any are still in business, or haunt your second-hand bookstores.

If you succeed in getting any of these magazines, please let us know. We'll pay you a handsome price for them.

Yours,
Ray Albert
President
Science Fiction Society

May 11, 1952

Mr. Sampson J. Gross, Editor
Strange Worlds Magazine
St. Louis, Mo.

Dear Mr. Gross:

I am enclosing the manuscript of a story I have just completed. As you see on the title page, I call it "Wreckers of Ten Million Galaxies." Because of the great amount of research that went into it, I must set the price on this one at not less than two cents a word.

Hoping you will see fit to use it in your magazine, I remain,

Respectfully,
Jack Lewis

May 19, 1952

Mr. Jack Lewis
90-26 219 St.
Queens Village, N.Y.

Dear Mr. Lewis:

I'm sorry, but at the present time we won't be able to use "Wreckers of Ten Million Galaxies." It's a great tale though, and if at some future date we decide to use it we will make out the check directly to the living relatives of Todd Thromberry.

That boy sure could write.

Cordially,
Sampson J. Gross
Editor
Strange Worlds Magazine

May 23, 1952

Mr. Doyle P. Gates, Editor
Deep Space Magazine
New York, N.Y.

Dear Mr. Gates:

While I said I would never have any dealings with you or your magazine again, something has happened which is most puzzling.

It seems all my stories are being returned to me by reason of the fact that except for my name, they are exact copies of the stories of this Todd Thromberry person.

In your last letter you described the odds on the accidental occurrence of this in the case of one story. What would you consider the odds on no less than half a dozen of my writings?

I agree with you—out of sight!

Yet in the interest of all humanity, how can I get the idea across to you that every word I have submitted was actually written *by me!* I have never copied any material from Todd Thromberry, nor have I ever seen any of his writings. In fact, as I told you in one of my letters, up until a short while ago I was totally unaware of his very existence.

An idea has occurred to me however. It's a truly weird idea, and one that I probably wouldn't even suggest to anyone but a science fiction editor. But suppose—just suppose—that this Thromberry person, what with his experiments in electricity and everything, had in some way managed to crack through this time-space barrier mentioned so often in your magazine. And suppose—conceited as it sounds—he had singled out my work as being the type of material he had always wanted to write.

Do you begin to follow me? Or is the idea of a person from a different time looking over my shoulder while I write too fantastic for you to accept?

Please write and tell me what you think of my idea.

Respectfully,
Jack Lewis

May 25, 1952

Mr. Jack Lewis
90-26 219 St.
Queens Village, N.Y.

Dear Mr. Lewis:

We think you should consult a psychiatrist.

Sincerely,
Doyle P. Gates
Science Fiction Editor
Deep Space Magazine

Mr. Sam Mines
Science Fiction Editor
Standard Magazines Inc.
New York 16, N.Y.

Dear Mr. Mines:

While the enclosed is not really a manuscript at all, I am submitting this series of letters, carbon copies, and correspondence, in the hope that you might give some belief to this seemingly unbelievable happening.

The enclosed letters are all in proper order and should explain themselves. Perhaps if you publish them, some of your readers might have some idea how all this could have happened.

I call the entire thing "Who's Cribbing?"

Respectfully,
Jack Lewis

June 10, 1952

Mr. Jack Lewis
90-26 219 St.
Queens Village, N.Y.

Dear Mr. Lewis:

Your idea of a series of letters to put across a science-fiction idea is an interesting one, but I'm afraid it doesn't quite come off.

It was in the August 1940 issue of *Macabre Adventures*

109

that Mr. Thromberry first used this very idea. Strangely enough, the story title also was "Who's Cribbing?"

Feel free to contact us again when you have something more original.

Yours,
Samuel Mines
Science Fiction Editor
Standard Magazines Inc.

Recall

1. Jack Lewis's troubles start when he (a) knowingly steals the writings of others (b) consults a psychiatrist (c) is accused by an editor of trying to sell someone else's story.
2. Todd Thromberry is (a) Jack Lewis before he legally changed his name (b) a writer who's been dead since 1941 (c) the president of the Science Fiction Society.
3. Twice in the story, Todd Thromberry is mentioned in connection with (a) atomic energy (b) electricity (c) improvement in automobile engines.
4. Who's cribbing? According to the editors, the answer to this question is (a) Todd Thromberry (b) Jack Lewis (c) nearly all writers of sci-fi.
5. At the end of the story, the mystery is (a) made even more mysterious (b) solved (c) turned over to the police.

Infer

6. One very unusual thing about "Who's Cribbing?" is that (a) there is a surprise at the end (b) the author uses himself as the main character (c) all the characters are men.
7. At no point in the story does the main character really seem (a) confused (b) angry (c) dishonest.
8. "Sir: Your accusations are typical of the rag you publish." It's clear from the story that *rag* means (a) paper made from rags (b) cloth-covered books (c) magazine.
9. One thing in the story that doesn't really make much sense is that (a) a writer becomes recognized only after his death (b) science fiction was being written nearly fifty years ago (c) Jack Lewis cannot find copies of stories that so many other people in the field seem to know about.
10. The surprise at the end is that (a) Todd Thromberry was alive as late as 1940 (b) the story "Who's Cribbing?" itself seems to have been written by Thromberry (c) the mystery is finally solved.

Vocabulary Review

Write on your paper the word in *italics* that belongs in each blank. Use each word only once.

accusation	*cribbing*	*occurrence*
barrier	*manuscript*	*plagiarism*

1. A person who wrongfully copies the writings of another can be accused of either —————— or ——————.
2. It is often hard to tell if a writer's —————— is really his own.
3. But the strict laws against stealing written material provide a pretty good —————— against its happening too often.
4. Students sometimes face the —————— that they have copied what they should have written themselves.
5. Do you know of a recent —————— of this in your school?

Critical Thinking

1. What is Jack Lewis's problem in the story? What steps does he take to try to solve this problem? Given the problem, do you think any of his reactions are unreasonable? Explain.

2. At one point in the story, Lewis wonders if Todd Thromberry "had in some way managed to crack through this time-space barrier" and "singled out my work as being the type of material he had always wanted to write." Explain in your own words what this means.

3. Have you ever read another story that was told as a series of letters? Why is the use of letters a particularly good idea for *this* story?

4. Think of another letter Jack Lewis could have written in the attempt to solve his problem. Write that letter and the reply. Indicate where your letters should be inserted in the story.

In Our Block

R. A. Lafferty

*There's no single word for the amazing R. A.
Lafferty. Zany doesn't quite fit. Neither does mad,
fantastic, funny, original, or clever. He's all of
these, and something more. He's a word wizard.
He's the court jester in the Science Fiction Hall of
Fame. He turns common sense into nonsense and
nonsense into fun. After reading this story, you
may find it easier to believe that he was born on
another planet and writes his stories backward on
a thought-typewriter while tying his shoelaces on
Thursday mornings.*

Vocabulary Preview

ASSEMBLE (uh SEM bul) to fit or join together
from parts
  • The bicycle came in a box and we had
  to *assemble* it at home.
CHUTE (SHOOT) a slide down which boxes
and other objects may pass
  • From the truck, the boxes went down
  the *chute* and into the store.
PIER (PEER) a strong post or pillar
  • Very small buildings are sometimes
  supported by *piers.*
SHANTY (SHAN tee) a shack; any small, old,
run-down building
  • The poor old man and his dog lived in a
  shanty.
STENOGRAPHER (stuh NOG ruh fur) a
secretary; a person skilled in shorthand
and typing
  • A secretary works for one company,
  but a public *stenographer* may work for
  anyone who will pay.
STOCK (STOK) supply; things kept for sale
  • That garage has the largest *stock* of
  tires in town.

Thehere were a lot of funny people in that block.

"You ever walk down that street?" Art Slick asked Jim Boomer, who had just come onto him there.

"Not since I was a boy. After the overall factory burned down, there was a faith healer had his tent there one summer. The street's just one block long and it's a dead end. Nothing but a bunch of shanties and weed-filled lots. The shanties looked different today, though. There seem to be more of them. I thought they pulled them all down a few months ago."

"Jim, I've been watching that first little building for two hours. There was a tractor-truck there this morning with a forty foot trailer, and it loaded out of that little shanty. Boxes about eight inches by eight inches by three foot came down that chute. They weighed about thirty-five pounds each, from the way the men handled them. Jim, they filled that trailer up with them, and then pulled it off."

"What's wrong with that, Art?"

"Jim, I said they filled that trailer up. It had about a sixty thousand pound load when it pulled out. They loaded a box every three and a half seconds for two hours; that's two thousand boxes."

"Sure, lots of trailers run over the load limit nowadays. They don't enforce it very well."

"Jim, that shack's no more than a cracker box seven feet on a side. Half of it is taken up by a door, and inside is a man in a chair behind a small table. You couldn't get anything else in that half. The other half is taken up by whatever that chute comes out of. You could pack six of those little shacks on that trailer."

"Let's measure it," Jim Boomer said. "Maybe it's bigger than it looks." The shack had a sign on it: MAKE SELL SHIP

115

ANYTHING CUT PRICE. Jim Boomer measured the building with an old steel tape. The shack was exactly seven by seven, and there were no hidden places. It was set up on a few piers of broken bricks, and you could see under it.

"Sell you a new fifty-foot steel tape for a dollar," said the man in the chair in the little shack. "Throw that old one away." The man pulled a steel tape out of a drawer of his table-desk, though Art Slick was sure it had been a plain flat-top table with no place for a drawer.

"Fully guaranteed, chrome plated. The best there is and it forms its own carrying case. One dollar," the man said.

Jim Boomer paid him a dollar for it. "How many of them you got?"

"I can have a hundred thousand ready to load out in ten minutes," the man said. "Eighty-eight cents each if you buy a hundred thousand."

"Was that a trailer-load of steel tapes you shipped out this morning?" Art asked the man.

"No, that must have been something else. This is the first steel tape I ever made. Just got the idea when I saw you measuring my shack with that old beat-up one."

Art Slick and Jim Boomer went to the run-down building next door. It was smaller, about six foot square, and the sign said PUBLIC STENOGRAPHER. The clatter of a typewriter was coming from it, but the noise stopped when they opened the door.

A dark, pretty girl was sitting in a chair before a small table. There was nothing else in the room, and no typewriter.

"I though I heard a typewriter in here," Art said.

"Oh, that is me," the girl smiled. "Sometimes I amuse myself make typewriter noises like a public stenographer is supposed to."

"What would you do if someone came in to have some typing done?"

"What are you think? I do it of course."

"Could you type a letter for me?"

"Sure is can, man friend, fifty cents a page, good work, carbon copy, envelope and stamp."

"Ah, let's see how you do it. I will dictate to you while you type."

"You dictate first. Then I write. No sense mix up two things at one time."

Art dictated a long and complicated letter that he had been meaning to write for several days. He felt like a fool dictating it to the girl as she filed her nails. "Why is public stenographer always sit filing her nails?" she asked as Art went on. "But I try to do it right, file them down, grow them out again, then file them down some more. Been doing it all morning. It seems silly."

"Ah—that is all," Art said when he had finished dictating.

"Not P.S. Love and Kisses?" the girl asked.

"Hardly. It's a business letter to a person I barely know."

"I always say P.S. Love and Kisses to persons I barely know," the girl said. "Your letter will make three pages, dollar fifty. Please you both step outside about ten seconds and I write it. Can't do it when you watch." She pushed them out and closed the door.

Then there was silence.

"What are you doing in there, girl?" Art called.

"Want I sell you a memory course too? You forget already? I type a letter," the girl called.

"But I don't hear a typewriter going."

"What is? You want the real sound too? I should charge extra." There was a giggle, and then the sound of very rapid typing for about five seconds.

The girl opened the door and handed Art the three page letter. It was typed perfectly, of course.

"There is something a little odd about this," Art said.

"Oh? The ungrammar of the letter is your own, sir. Should I have correct?"

"No. It is something else. Tell me the truth, girl—how does the man next door ship out trailer-loads of things from a building ten times too small to hold the stuff?"

"He cuts prices."

"Well, what are you people? The man next door looks like you."

"My brother-uncle. We tell every body we are Innominee Indians."

"There is no such tribe," Jim Boomer said flatly.

"Is there not? Then we will have to tell people we are something else. You got to admit it sounds like Indian. What's the best Indian to be?"

"Shawnee," said Jim Boomer.

"O.K. then we be Shawnee Indians. See how easy it is."

"We're already taken," Boomer said. "I'm a Shawnee and I know every Shawnee in town."

"Hi, cousin!" the girl cried, and winked. "That's from a joke I learn, only the begin was different. See how foxy I turn all your questions."

"I have two quarters in change coming," Art said.

"I know," the girl said. "I forgot for a minute what design is on the back of the two-bitser piece, so I stall while I remember it. Yes, the funny bird standing on the bundle of fire wood. One moment till I finish them. Here." She handed the quarters to Art Slick. "And you tell everybody there's a smoothie public stenographer here who types letters good."

"Without a typewriter," said Art Slick. "Let's go, Jim."

"P.S. Love and Kisses," the girl called after them.

The Cool Man Club was next door, a small and shabby beer bar. The bar girl could have been a sister of the public stenographer.

"We'd like a couple of bottles of Budweiser but you don't seem to have a stock of anything," Art said.

"Who needs stock?" the girl asked. "Here is beers." Art would have believed that she brought them out of her sleeves, but she had no sleeves. The beers were cold and good.

"Girl, do you know how the fellow on the corner can ship a whole trailer-load of stuff out of a space, like if he made it before time."

"But he has to make it out of something," Jim Boomer cut in.

"No, no," the girl said. "I study your language. I know words. Out of something is to assemble, not to make. He makes."

"This is funny," Slick gaped. "Budweiser is spelled wrong on this bottle, the i before the e."

"Oh, I goof," the bar girl said. "I couldn't remember which way it goes so I make it one way on one bottle and the other way on the other. Yesterday a man ordered a bottle of Progress beer, and I spelled it Progers on the bottle. Sometimes I get things wrong. Here, I fix yours."

She ran her hand over the label, and then it was spelled correctly.

"But that thing is carefully printed somewhere," Slick protested.

"Oh, sure, all fancy stuff like that," the girl said. "I got to be more careful. One time I forgot and make Jax-taste beer in a Schlitz bottle and the man didn't like it. I had to swish swish change the taste while I pretended to give him a different bottle. 'It is the light in here, it just makes it look brown,' I told the man. Hell, we don't even have a light in here. I go swish fast and make the bottle green. It's hard to keep from making mistake when you're stupid."

"No, you don't have a light or a window in here, and it's light," Slick said. "You don't have a refrigerator. There's no

119

electricity in any of the shanties in this block. How do you keep the beer cold?"

"Yes, is the beer not nice and cold? Notice how tricky I get out of your question. Will you good men have two more beers?"

"Yes, we will. And I'm interested in seeing where you will get them," Slick said.

"Oh look, is snakes behind you!" the girl cried.

"Oh how you jump!" she laughed. "It's all joke. Do you think I will have snakes in my nice bar?"

But she had produced two more beers, and the place was as bare as before.

"How long have you folks been in this block?" Boomer asked.

"Who keep track?" the girl said. "People come and go."

"You're not from around here," Slick said. "You're not from anywhere I know. Where do you come from? Mars? Jupiter?"

"Who wants Jupiter?" the girl seemed angry. "Do business with a bunch of insects there is all! Freeze your tail too."

"You wouldn't be a kidder, would you, girl?" Slick asked.

"I sure do try hard. I learn a lot of jokes but I tell them all wrong yet. I get better, though. I try to be the funny bar girl so people will come back."

"What's in the shanty next door to the tracks?"

"My cousin-sister," said the girl. "She set up shop just today. She grow any color hair on bald-headed men. I tell her she's crazy. No business. If they wanted hair they wouldn't be bald-headed in the first place."

"Well, *can* she grow hair on baldheaded men?" Slick asked.

"Oh sure. Can't you?"

120

There were three or four more shanty shops in the block. It didn't seem that there had been that many when the men went into *The Cool Man Club.*

"I don't remember seeing this shack a few minutes ago," Boomer said to the man standing in front of the last shanty on the line.

"Oh, I just made it," the man said.

Old gray boards, rusty nails . . . and he had just made it.

"Why didn't you—ah—make a decent building while you were at it?" Slick asked.

"This fits in better," the man said. "Who notices when an *old* building appears suddenly? We're new here and want to feel our way in before we attract attention. Now I'm trying to figure out what to make. Do you think there are people who would buy a luxury automobile for a hundred dollars? I suspect I would have to pay attention to the local religious feeling when I make them, though."

"What is that?" Slick asked.

"Ancestor worship. The old gas tank and fuel system still carried, even after natural power is available. Oh, well, I'll put them in. I'll have one done in about three minutes if you want to wait."

"No. I already got a car," Slick said. "Let's go, Jim."

That was the last shanty in the block, so they turned back.

"I just got to wondering what was down in this block where nobody ever goes," Slick said. "There's a lot of odd corners in our town if you look them out."

"There were some queer guys in the row of shanties that were here before this bunch," Boomer said. "Some of them used to come up to the *Red Rooster* to drink. One of them could gobble like a turkey. One of them could roll one eye in

121

one direction and the other eye the other way. They worked at the cotton-seed oil factory before it burned down."

They went by the public stenographer shack again.

"No kidding, honey, how do you type without a typewriter?" Slick asked.

"Typewriter is too slow," the girl said.

"I asked How, not Why," Slick said.

"I know. Is it not clever the way I turn away a sentence? I think I will have a big oak tree growing in front of my shop tomorrow for shade. Either of you nice men have an acorn in your pocket?"

"Ah—no. How do you really do the typing, girl?"

"You promise you won't tell anybody."

"I promise."

"I make the marks with my tongue," the girl said.

They started slowly on up the block.

"Hey, how do you make the carbon copies?" Jim Boomer called back.

"With my other tongue," the girl said.

There was another forty-foot trailer loading out of the first shanty in the block. It was bundles of half-inch pipe coming out of the chute—in twenty foot lengths. Twenty foot pipe out of a seven foot shed.

"I wonder how he can sell trailer-loads of such stuff out of a little shack like that," Slick puzzled, still not satisfied.

"Like the girl says, he cuts prices," Boomer said. "Let's go over to the *Red Rooster* and see if there's anything going on. There always were a lot of funny people in that block."

Recall

1. In the beginning of the story, Art Slick tells of his amazement at (a) a new car for $100 (b) all the boxes that came out of a small shack (c) a public stenographer's speed.

2. The bar girl, the public stenographer, and the man in the shack all (a) have red hair (b) are Shawnee Indians (c) can do amazing things.

3. In order, Slick and Boomer spend money on (a) a steel tape, beer, a typing job (b) a typing job, a steel tape, beer (c) a steel tape, a typing job, beer.

4. In addition to the man in the shack, the public stenographer, and the bar girl, Slick and Boomer also talk to (a) a woman who grows hair on bald-headed men (b) a woman who tells fortunes (c) a man who has just made a new-old shack.

5. At the end of the story, Slick and Boomer go off to (a) tell the police (b) see what else is going on in town (c) get some money and come back.

Infer

6. The reply "He cuts prices" is funny because (a) it completely ignores the purpose of the question (b) the prices were actually raised (c) *cuts* is a strange word to use for "lowers."

7. There's a suggestion in the story that the people in the block (a) will someday take over the world (b) come from outer space (c) have a large factory underground.

8. The bar girl discusses the difference in meaning between *assembles* and *makes*. To her, *makes* means (a) puts together from parts (b) creates (c) forces.

9. The amazing thing about Slick and Boomer is that they (a) are very surprised at the strange events (b) aren't at all surprised at the strange events (c) aren't surprised enough at the strange events.

10. It is clear from the story that its author, R. A. Lafferty, has a keen sense of (a) justice (b) smell (c) the ridiculous.

Vocabulary Review

1. If a store clerk tells you that a certain item is out of *stock,* he means that (a) it's out of style (b) his supply has run out (c) the factory that makes it is on strike.
2. The *shanty* was set on *piers.* In other words the (a) song was set on a piano (b) shack was set on fire (c) shack was supported by posts.
3. You'd be most likely to find a *chute* in back of a (a) supermarket (b) jewelry store (c) doctor's office.
4. A person whose job it is to *assemble* things probably works in a (a) school (b) factory (c) supermarket.

Critical Thinking

1. What kind of people are Art Slick and Jim Boomer? How does this add to the story?
2. If you had only five words to describe the characters who live in the block, what would they be? Try to think of *exact* words, not terms like "unusual."
3. The character who says he can make a new car in three minutes speaks of "natural power." What does he mean?
4. Some readers miss part of the fun in "In Our Block" because they don't get some of the jokes. Explain in your own words why each of the following is amusing:

   The public stenographer: "He cuts prices."

   The bar girl: "It's hard to keep from making mistakes when you're stupid."

   Jim Boomer: "There always were a lot of funny people on that block."
5. In the language of science fiction, people from other planets who come to Earth are known as *aliens.* How does "In Our Block" differ from most other stories about aliens?

   124

The Room

Ray Russell

Did you ever groan about all the commercials on TV? Did you ever feel like calling newspapers "adpapers"? Did you ever feel boxed-in by billboards? Did you ever curse a singing commercial that got stuck in the record groove of your mind? Did you ever think that the whole world was becoming filled with advertising? If so, you're exactly the person who should love the following story.

Bob Crane lives in a future world that really is filled with advertising. A "Sleepcoo" voice whispers commercials throughout the night, and a "Projecto" machine flashes ads on his walls and ceiling. He sees ads everywhere, even on the backs of $5.00 bills. And finally, he decides to do something to get away from the ads. If you're normal, maybe you'd do just the same thing. . .

125

Vocabulary Preview

COMPETITOR (kum PET uh tur) one who
competes; an opponent
  • Burger King and Gino's are *competitors*
  of MacDonalds.

DECISIVE (dih SIE siv) quick at deciding
  • Ms. Massameno is a *decisive* teacher
  who wastes little classroom time.

FRUITLESS (FROOT less) unsuccessful;
useless
  • Heather looked everywhere, but her
  search was *fruitless.*

HESITANT (HEZ uh tunt) slow to decide or to
act
  • Some people are so *hesitant* that they
  almost never decide on anything.

JINGLE (JING gul) a simple, catchy tune or
poem
  • Many TV commercials contain *jingles*
  that help you remember the product.

LOGY (LOW gee) tired; having no energy
  • After feeling *logy* for weeks, Ms.
  Thorpe went to her doctor.

CRANE AWOKE WITH THE TINGLE TOOTH-foam song racing through his head. Tingle, he realized, must have bought last night's Sleepcoo time. He frowned at the Sleepcoo speaker in the wall next to his pillow. Then he stared at the ceiling: it was still blank. Must be pretty early, he told himself. As the Coffizz slogan slowly faded in on the ceiling, he turned his eyes away and got out of bed. He avoided looking at the printed messages on the sheets, the pillowcases, the blankets, his robe, and the innersoles of his slippers. As his feet touched the floor, the TV set went on. It would go off, automatically, at ten P.M. Crane was perfectly free to switch channels, but he saw no point in that.

In the bathroom, he turned on the light and the TV's sound was immediately piped in to him. He switched the light off and stood there in the dark. But he needed light in order to shave, and as he turned it on again, the sound resumed. As he shaved, the mirror flickered once every three seconds. It was not enough to disturb his shaving, but Crane found himself suddenly thinking of the rich warm goodness of the Coffizz competitor, Teatang. A few moments later, he was reading other ads which were printed on sheets of the bathroom tissue.

As he was dressing, the phone rang. He let it ring. He knew what he would hear if he picked it up: "Good morning!

127

Have you had your Krakkeroonies yet? Packed with protein and ——'' Or, maybe, "Why wait? Enlist now in the service of your choice and cash in on the following enlistee benefits— —'' Or: "Feeling under the weather? Heart disease kills four out of five! The early symptoms are——''

On the other hand, it *could* be an important personal call. He picked up the phone and said hello. "Hello yourself," answered a husky feminine voice. "Bob?"

"Yes."

"Bob Crane?"

"Yes, who's this?"

"My name's Judy. I know you, but you don't know me. Have you felt logy lately, out of sorts——'' He put down the phone. That settled it. He pulled a crumpled slip of paper from his desk drawer. There was an address on it. Before, he had been hesitant about following up this lead. But this morning he felt decisive. He left his apartment and hailed a cab.

The back of the cab's front seat immediately went on and he found himself watching the Juice-O-Vescent Breakfast Hour. He opened a newspaper the last passenger had left behind. His eyes managed to slide over the four-color Glitter-ink ads, and he tried to concentrate on a news story about another government housing program, but his attempts to ignore the Breeze Deodorant ads printed yellow-on-white be-tween the lines were fruitless. The cab reached its destina-tion. Crane paid the driver with a bill bearing a picture of Abraham Lincoln on one side and a picture of a woman ba-thing with Smoothie Soap on the other. He entered a rather run-down building, found the correct door, and pressed the doorbell. He could hear, inside, the sound of an old-fash-ioned buzzer, not a chime playing the EetMeet or Jetfly or Krispy Kola jingles. Hope filled him.

128

A tired dirty woman answered the door, regarded him suspiciously, and asked, "Yeah?"

"I—uh—Mrs. Ferman? I got your name from a friend, Bill Seavers? I understand you—" his voice dropped low "—rent rooms."

"Get outta here; you wanna get me in trouble? I'm a private citizen, a respectable——"

"I'll, I'll *pay*. I have a good job. I——"

"How much?"

"Two hundred? That's twice what I'm paying at the housing project."

"Come on in." Inside, the woman locked and chained the door. "One room," she said. "Toilet and shower down the hall, you share it with two others. Get rid of your own garbage. Provide your own heat in the winter. You want hot water, it's fifty extra. No cooking in the rooms. No guests. Three months' rent in advance, cash."

"I'll take it," Crane said quickly; then added, "I can turn off the TV?"

"There ain't no TV. No phone neither."

"No all-night Sleepcoo next to the bed? No ads in the mirrors? No Projecto in the ceiling or walls?"

"None of that stuff."

Crane smiled. He counted out the rent into her dirty hand. "When can I move in?"

She shrugged. "Any time. Here's the key. Fourth floor, front. There ain't no elevator."

Crane left, still smiling, the key clutched in his hand.

Mrs. Ferman picked up the phone and dialed a number. "Hello?" she said. "Ferman reporting. We have a new one, male, about thirty."

"Fine, thank you," answered a voice. "Begin treatment at once, Dr. Ferman."

129

Recall

1. The story probably takes place during (a) an hour or two (b) a day (c) a week or more.
2. Bob Crane wakes up in a world filled with (a) threats of war (b) hunger and starvation (c) commercials and ads.
3. Crane lets the phone ring awhile because he (a) is in the bathroom (b) thinks it might be someone selling something (c) doesn't want to talk to Judy again.
4. Crane had gotten the address of the room from (a) a friend (b) an ad in a newspaper (c) the back of a $5.00 bill.
5. Crane decides to rent the room because it is (a) cheaper (b) nearer his office (c) free of ads and commercials.
6. The "tired, dirty woman" who rents Crane the room turns out to be (a) a doctor (b) as poor as she looks (c) someone who knew Crane previously.

Infer

7. The room itself turns out to be (a) a great bargain (b) a kind of trap (c) too large for Crane's needs.
8. The "treatment" mentioned at the end of the story will probably (a) make Crane happy with a simple life (b) cure any physical disease he might have (c) change his feelings about commercials and ads.
9. Judged by the standards of *his own* society, Bob Crane is (a) superior (b) intelligent (c) not normal.
10. Judged by the standards of *our* society, Bob Crane is (a) a normal person (b) a saint (c) an adventurer.

Vocabulary Review

Write on your paper the word in *italics* that belongs in each blank. Use each word only once.

competitor
decisive
fruitless
hesitant
jingle
logy

1. When I was a freshman, I felt —————— about joining the track team.
2. As a sophomore, however, I felt —————— enough to join.
3. Jill Rooney was my only real —————— in the 880-yard race.
4. On try-out day she had a cold and felt ——————, so I won easily.
5. I don't think when I run; I just keep repeating some advertising —————— to myself.
6. I've tried the high jump too, but my efforts have been —————.

Critical Thinking

1. In your own world of today, what kind of advertising makes you most angry? Why do you think you get so annoyed with it? Explain your answer carefully.

131

2. How many of the kinds of advertising mentioned in the story are new to you? Think of at least three. Can you think of any possible kind of advertising that the story does not mention? Try to come up with at least one.

3. The story is an effective one because it really does "pile horror upon horror." The description of advertising methods is horrible enough. But the really shocking horror comes at the end, in the last two paragraphs. Explain the idea about the future that makes the ending of the story such a horror.

So You Too Can Write Sci-fi?

K. Ripke, L. Leigh, T. Bruey

A few years ago, writer Fredric Brown (see "Something Green," page 161) set himself a problem:

The last man on Earth sat alone in a room. There was a knock at the door . . .

In a short story written to solve the problem, Brown proved that the three dots at the end need not lead to the horror they hint at. In fact, in Brown's solution to the problem, the knock comes as the happiest of endings.

But what about the problem? Who could have knocked? A Martian? The last woman on Earth? The branch of a tree? You decide, quickly!

Vocabulary Preview

CYANIDE (SI uh nide) a deadly poison
  • *Cyanide* is sometimes used to kill woodchucks, coyotes, and other animals.
ERODE (ih RODE) to eat or wear away, as rain does to soil
  • Polluted air and rain water can *erode* even the strongest concrete.
GENERATOR (JEN uh ray tur) a machine that makes electricity
  • Some people own a *generator* for use when the power goes off.
HIDE (HIDE) the skin of an animal
  • Some shoes are made of a cow's *hide.*
SCAVENGER (SKAV un gur) a person (or animal) who lives on what he can find
  • After the war, Tang Lee had to become a *scavenger* to stay alive.
SINUS (SI nus) having to do with the small openings in the bone of the forehead
  • People with *sinus* trouble often have runny noses and headaches.
SURVIVOR (sur VI vur) a person who survives, or lives through, a danger
  • The *survivors* of the plane crash were rushed to the hospital.

Okay, HERE'S A TEST:
The last man on Earth sat alone in a room. There was a knock at the door . . .

YOU HAVE EXACTLY ONE HOUR OF HOME-WORK TIME TO WRITE THE STORY. It must include the two *italicized* sentences above. They can come at the beginning, the middle, or the end, but they must be included.

A hard assignment? Not really. Haven't you ever read a story and then said to yourself, "Oh, I could do better than that, if I really wanted to try." SO TRY! Just think of a good solution to the problem, and write it out. Include plenty of details to make it seem real.

Three solutions written by students follow. Please don't start reading till you can compare your story against them. Who knows? Yours might be better!

SOLUTION I

"Ah, warmth at last." After trying for three days, Erod finally managed to get the generator going. It hadn't been easy piecing the scattered metal parts together. It had been even harder to make sense of the tattered instruction book. He had nearly given up a hundred times, but his basic urge to go on living had won out in the end. Or had it? "Why bother trying?" Erod thought aloud. "No one will know, no one will care if I live or die." It wasn't easy being the only living survivor of the Last War. Even if one could ignore the smell of dead bodies and still-smoking fires, life would always be a nightmare. No conversation. No companionship. Never again to feel the warmth of human love.

On the edge of madness for the first few weeks, the last

135

living man searched in vain for others who might still be alive. Anybody, or even a dog or a cat, would have been welcome relief. Things were a little better now. The generator was working; he had heat, lights, music. And he'd been lucky enough to find a house still standing. The days were filled with scavenger hunts, hard work, and hope. The nights were horrors of doubts, hopelessness, and terror-filled dreams. One in particular returned to haunt him. He was standing in the driveway waving good by to his kids. Driving to work, everyone turned to glare at him. He wondered if the people knew about his top-secret work. "Impossible," he exclaimed. But if the public ever found out about the Zenox Automatic Bomb he'd developed, there would be trouble, real trouble. On Erod's desk was a secret letter from the government. Greenland had discovered the bomb. A stern warning had been issued. Destroy it or be destroyed. *Destroy it or be destroyed.* DESTROY IT OR BE DESTROYED. He awoke every night at this point. The government had tried to ignore the warning, and early the next day the first bombs had been dropped. "Must be loser's luck," he said to himself. "I'm the only man left alive, and it's all my fault."

Winter slowly moved in. The hunts had to be delayed till spring. The nights grew longer, colder, harder to get through. The dreams grew more frightening. Loneliness became his constant companion. The pieces of furniture, the pictures on the walls, the doorknobs were transformed into silent roommates. In a fit of discouragement, Erod turned to his one escape. A cyanide pill slid gently down his throat. Smiling peacefully for the first time in months, Erod thought, "I'll be home soon."

The last man on Earth sat alone in a room. There was a knock at the door . . .

—Karen Ripke

136

SOLUTION II

The last man on Earth sat alone in a room. There was a knock at the door. The man sat still and quiet. There was another knock at the door.

"Who the —?" he thought to himself.

Finally he got up enough courage to go and answer it. He rose to his feet and slowly made his way across the dirt-filled room. The strong smell of animal hide made him cough.

"Quiet, you fool!" he scolded himself.

When he reached the door, he put his right hand on the knob. Then he put his left hand on a small whip that was lying on a black table.

There was another knock, this time so loud that it startled him. Every nerve in his body twitched at once. A large drop of perspiration ran down his forehead and into his right eye. He took his right hand off the doorknob and wiped his eye.

"Who is it?" he whispered to the door.

No one answered.

"Who is it?" he said again.

"Polly want a cracker," came the reply from outside.

Relieved, the man opened the door and let the bird in. He put his whip down.

Polly was a small bird with large blue feathers and an enormous bill. The man held out a cracker taken from his pocket. It disappeared in an instant into the bird's beak.

"There," said the man as he reached to close the door.

"How about me?" came a voice from outside the room. It was another parrot. The man gave the other bird a cracker and the two flew away together.

"Nice little birds," thought the man. "Not like those alligators and snakes downstairs. Yick, I hate them so! But what can I do? I have to feed them now, anyway."

137

He grabbed a large cloth sack and his whip and walked from the room, closing the door carefully behind him. He proceeded down a long corridor and down a tall winding staircase. Finally he reached the place where the animals were. He filled the sack with raw meat he had collected earlier. This he carried to the pits that held the meat-eating animals. He threw the meat in and stood watching the animals devour it. Then he cleaned his hands with water in a large pan and went on to feed the less dangerous animals.

"What a task!" he repeated over and over again to himself. After about seven hours he finished.

"Thank G—," he began. "Oh, I shouldn't have said that," he thought aloud. "Well, finally I'm done for the day."

All of a sudden his whole small world began to shake. He grabbed for a small chair that was nailed to the floor and held on. Soon all was quiet.

"Could it be . . .?" he wondered.

"No, it couldn't," he continued. He ran upstairs to his room and lifted the lid on a small wooden desk. He counted the times he had fed the animals.

"Could it be . . .?" he though again. "Yes, it must be!" Without wasting a second, he grabbed everything in his small room that he could carry and kicked the door open with his foot. Down the corridor he ran, as fast as he could, and down the staircase. Finally he reached a large square door, thirty feet high. He threw down his arm load of belongings and sorted through them until he found his ax. Up the stairs he ran again and down to the opposite end of the corridor, where he hadn't been in a little over a month. He opened a small door and came upon two strong cables. He began chopping at the smaller one.

"I don't believe it. I have to move quickly. Quickly. Quickly." After about five minutes the small cable broke.

An ear-splitting squeak sounded as the pulleys up near the ceiling turned as they had so long ago.

The man began chopping at the other cable. This one was stronger, made of tough vines. Suddenly the ax handle snapped.

"No!" he screamed. "My only ax!"

He sat down on the floor and began to think. "After all this time, I can't waste another second." All at once his eyes lit up. "The elephants!" he exclaimed. He sprang to his feet, ran down the hall, flew down the stairs. He ran to the elephants' cage and grabbed the cable that had fallen from the ceiling when he had cut the other end with his ax. This he tied to the large cable that ran overhead. The other end he attached to the elephants' trunks.

"Back!" he yelled. "Back! Back! Back!"

Slowly the elephants moved backwards. The pulleys began to squeak as the cables grew tighter and tighter.

Bang! A large pulley broke from the wall. The large uncut cable fell from the ceiling. The man grabbed hold of one of the elephant's trunks as the whole large room shook. Beams began to break as all the remaining cables now moved at once. Then all was quiet. . . .

A loud, tearing sound broke the silence. One whole side of the room fell out.

All the animals began to make noise as the man opened the cages.

The man was the first one out into their new world.

A loud rumble shook the ground. The man stepped aside. Out rushed the animals.

"Thank you, Noah," came a thunder-like voice from above.

"You're welcome, my Lord," the man whispered as he fell to his knees in prayer.   —Louis Leigh (with apologies to Shem, Ham, and Japeth)

SOLUTION III

In the year 2000, on the last day of June, something strange was happening in the planet Earth. A blue-green gas was hanging over the planet. This gas had a very severe effect on human beings. Whenever a person breathed in some of it, he was turned into a stone.

It all started when the factory which made food pills for all of the people blew up. When this happened some of the pills flew into the smokestack of a nearby cement factory. When the pills burned they gave off the green gas. The repairmen tried to clean out the stack,but they were turned to concrete. The gas spread quickly and turned everyone into concrete. Everyone except one man.

This man was Mortimer Salvitore. He was a shoe salesman from Toledo, Ohio. He had been cursed all of his life with a severe sinus problem which made it very difficult for him to breathe deeply. This is what saved him from the gas. But he soon was wishing it hadn't saved him, because business had always been bad enough, and now stones and lumps of concrete couldn't wear shoes.

So the last man on Earth, Mortimer Salvitore, sat alone in a room with a suitcase full of samples, trying to think of what he should do. Suddenly there came a knock at the door. This startled Mort, first of all because no one had ever come to visit him before, and secondly because he was the last man on Earth. He ran to the door to find only a woodpecker making holes.

That's the way life was for Mort; he was a born loser. But now suddenly he thought of something. If he saved all the people in the world, then they'd be obliged to buy shoes from him. What a sales idea! Almost immediately a definite plan came to him. First he must shut off the cement factory.

Quickly Mort ran to the control of the factory, yet he

knew nothing about the plant. He ran around frantically in the green cloud looking for the shut-off switch. In the fog he didn't see an extension cord and tripped, losing his glasses. But in tripping he unplugged the factory. When he found his glasses and put them on, he realized the air had cleared.

Now all that was left to do was un-cement the people. This would seem impossible, except that Mort in all of his years as a shoe salesman had walked down many cracked sidewalks. These cracks, he knew, were made by salt. Mort rushed to every grocery store in the city and bought all the salt he could find. (Of course, being an honest citizen he left IOU's). He then dumped all of this salt on his next-door neighbor, who happened to be one of the world's greatest scientists. Then he waited for the rain. Again, the last man on Earth sat alone and waited.

The rain did come finally. Mort watched as it dissolved the salt, eroding the cement. The scientist was now free, and Mort explained the whole story. The scientist then developed a chemical that made Mort's salt work faster on the rest of the people. Mort had saved the people of the world! And they all lived happily ever after.

Except Mort. He sold lots of shoes, but being a born loser, he also got bills for the salt, which took him the rest of his life to pay.

—Tim Bruey

Recall

1. In "Solution I," Erod finds himself alone on Earth because of (a) a new and deadly disease (b) a war (c) an invasion from outer space.

141

2. At the end of "Solution I," Erod (a) finally fixes the broken generator (b) is saved by the knock at the door (c) kills himself.

3. In "Solution II" (Noah), the knock at the door is made by (a) a woman (b) an elephant (c) a parrot.

4. In "Solution II" (Noah), the purpose of all the cables is to (a) tie up the animals (b) open a large door (c) make the pulleys squeak.

5. In "Solution II," Noah solves the problem of the broken ax by using (a) a generator (b) parrots (c) elephants.

6. In "Solution III," Mortimer Salvitore finds himself the last man on Earth because of a (a) knowledge of good hiding places (b) flood (c) sinus problem.

7. In "Solution III," Mort's plan to save the world depends on (a) a pill (b) an ax (c) salt.

Infer

8. In "Solution I" (Erod), the knock at the end is probably made by (a) another survivor (b) a creature from outer space (c) an animal.

9. In "Solution II" (Noah), the "elephants" mentioned probably numbered (a) two (b) about five (c) in the hundreds.

10. In "Solution III," Mortimer might have lived to a happier old age if he had not been so (a) clever (b) honest (c) popular.

Vocabulary Review

1. A *generator* would be useful if you had no (a) food (b) school in your community (c) electricity.
2. The ham sandwich also contained *cyanide.* The person who ate it probably (a) said, *"yum!"* (b) asked for salt (c) died.
3. The *survivor* became a *scavenger.* In other words the (a) religious leader turned into a hero (b) one who still lived had to hunt for food (c) doctor became money hungry.
4. A person with *sinus* problems might do well to see a (a) loan agency (b) divorce lawyer (c) doctor.
5. Salty slush on the sidewalks will *erode* the best *hides.* In other words, the slush will (a) eat away the best leather (b) make it hard to find hiding places (c) hinder the best policemen.

Critical Thinking

1. How was the knock made in each of the three stories? In which one does it really have nothing to do with the story? Considering the instructions, do you think this is fair on the writer's part? Explain.
2. Which two of the stories depend on a surprise ending? In which of these must the end come as a *complete* surprise? In which is the ending indicated by several clues? What are some of these clues?

143

3. The stories were written by students in a limited period of time. None of the students took time to think of a title. Think of the best title you can for each. Remember, your title must not give away the ending.

4. Which story did you think was the best? Why? Try to think of at least three reasons. Use details in your answer; don't say things like "more interesting."

5. The three stories were all written by amateur writers like yourself. How do they differ from the other stories in this book, all of which were written by professionals? Be exact in your answer.

6. After the end of "Solution II," it reads "With apologies to Shem, Ham, and Japheth." Why? If you have no idea, get a Bible and look at *Genesis,* 7:13.

Examination Day

Henry Slesar

*The next story is set far in the future. The events it
describes will almost certainly never happen. It's
not a pleasant story, and you're not expected to
enjoy every word. When you finish, you'll say
something like "Ugh!" or "Horrible!" or "Yuk!"
or "I'll forget that one as soon as I can!"
And there's the catch. You won't be able to forget
"Examination Day." It may leave a bad taste in
your mouth, but it'll also leave an interesting
subject in your mind. You'll find yourself thinking
about that subject. Before long you may actually
be glad you read the story. So take a few deep
breaths—and plunge in.*

Vocabulary Preview

ATTENDANT (uh TEN dunt) a person who
attends, or waits on, others
• On weekends my brother works as a gas
station *attendant*.

COMPUTING (kum PEW ting) figuring;
determining; thinking
• Large *computing* machines can do
complicated math problems in seconds.

CONSISTENCY (kun SIS tun see) thickness or
firmness
• The cheap pancake syrup had the
consistency of water.

MULTI-DIALED (MULL tih DI uld) having
many dials or knobs
• Karen owns an expensive *multi-dialed*
hi-fi set.

SEQUENCE (SEE quens) order or arrangement
• Even numbers follow the *sequence*
2,4,6,8,10, . . .

SPECULATE (SPEK yuh late) to guess or try to
figure what's going to happen
• You can *speculate* about the future, but
you can never be sure.

THE JORDANS NEVER SPOKE OF THE EXAM, not until their son, Dickie, was twelve years old. It was on his birthday that Mrs. Jordan first mentioned the subject in his presence, and the anxious manner of her speech caused her husband to answer sharply.

"Forget about it," he said. "He'll do all right."

They were at the breakfast table, and the boy looked up from his plate curiously. He was an alert-eyed youngster, with flat blond hair and a quick, nervous manner. He didn't understand what the sudden trouble was about, but he did know that today was his birthday, and he wanted a happy day above all. Somewhere in the little apartment there were wrapped packages waiting to be opened, and in the tiny wall-kitchen, something warm and sweet was being prepared in the automatic stove. He wanted the day to be happy, and the moistness of his mother's eyes, the scowl on his father's face, spoiled the good mood with which he had greeted the morning.

"What exam?" he asked.

His mother looked at the tablecloth. "It's just a sort of Government intelligence test they give children at the age of twelve. You'll be getting it next week. It's nothing to worry about."

"You mean a test like in school?"

"Something like that," his father said, getting up from the table. "Go read your comic books, Dickie."

The boy rose and wandered toward that part of the living room which had always been "his" corner. He fingered the topmost comic of the stack, but seemed uninterested in the colorful squares of fast-paced action. He wandered toward the window, and peered gloomily at the mist outside the glass.

147

"Why did it have to rain *today?*" he said. "Why couldn't it rain tomorrow?"

His father, now slumped into an armchair with the Government newspaper, rattled the sheets suddenly. "Because it just did, that's all. Rain makes the grass grow."

"Why, Dad?"

"Because it does, that's all."

Dickie wrinkled up his brow. "What makes it green, though? The grass?"

"Nobody knows," his father snapped, then immediately regretted the tone of his voice.

Later in the day, it was birthday time again. His mother beamed as she handed over the gaily-colored packages, and even his father managed a grin and a rumple-of-the-hair. He kissed his mother and shook hands with his father. Then the birthday cake was brought forth, and the ceremonies ended.

An hour later, seated by the window, he watched the sun force its way between the clouds.

"Dad," he said, "how far away is the sun?"

"Five thousand miles," his father said.

Dick sat at the breakfast table and again saw moisture in his mother's eyes. He didn't connect her tears with the exam until his father suddenly brought the subject to light again.

"Well, Dickie," he said, with a manly frown, "you've got an appointment today."

"I know, Dad. I hope——"

"Now it's nothing to worry about. Thousands of children take this test every day. The Government wants to know how smart you are, Dickie. That's all there is to it."

"I get good marks in school," he said.

"This is different. This is a—special kind of test. They give you this stuff to drink, you see, and then you go into a room where there's a sort of machine——"

"What stuff to drink?" Dickie said.

"It's nothing. It tastes like peppermint. It's just to make sure you answer the questions truthfully. Not that the Government thinks you won't tell the truth, but this stuff makes *sure.*"

Dickie's face showed puzzlement, and a touch of fright. He looked at his mother, and she arranged her face into a misty smile.

"Everything will be all right," she said.

"Of course it will," his father agreed. "You're a good boy, Dickie; you'll make out fine. Then we'll come home and celebrate. All right?"

"Yes, sir," Dickie said.

They entered the Government Educational Building fifteen minutes before the appointed hour. They crossed the marble floors of the great lobby, passed beneath an archway and entered an automatic elevator that brought them to the fourth floor.

There was a young man wearing a uniform, seated at a polished desk in front of Room 404. He held a clipboard in his hand, and he checked the list down to the Js and permitted the Jordans to enter.

The room was as cold and official as a courtroom, with long benches and metal tables. There were several fathers and sons already there, and a thin-lipped woman with short black hair was passing out sheets of paper.

Mr. Jordan filled out the form, and returned it to the clerk. Then he told Dickie: "It won't be long now. When they call your name, you just go through the doorway at that end of the room." He indicated the door with his finger.

A loudspeaker crackled and called off the first name. Dickie saw a boy leave his father's side and walk slowly toward the door.

At five minutes of eleven they called the name of Jordan.

"Good luck, son," his father said, without looking at him. "I'll call for you when the test is over."

Dickie walked to the door and turned the knob. The room inside was dim, and he could barely make out the features of the uniformed attendant who greeted him.

"Sit down," the man said softly. He indicated a high stool beside his desk. "Your name's Richard Jordan?"

"Yes, sir."

"Your classification number is 600-115. Drink this, Richard."

He lifted a plastic cup from the desk and handed it to the boy. The liquid inside had the consistency of buttermilk, tasted only vaguely of the promised peppermint. Dickie downed it, and handed the man the empty cup.

He sat in silence, feeling a little sleepy, while the man wrote busily on a sheet of paper. Then the attendant looked at his watch, and rose to stand only inches from Dickie's face. He unclipped a pen-like object from his pocket, and flashed a tiny light into the boy's eyes.

"All right," he said. "Come with me, Richard."

He led Dickie to the end of the room, where a single wooden armchair faced a multi-dialed computing machine. There was a microphone on the left arm of the chair, and when the boy sat down, he found its pinpoint head conveniently at his mouth.

"Now just relax, Richard. You'll be asked some questions, and you think them over carefully. Then give your answers into the microphone. The machine will take care of the rest."

"Yes, sir."

"I'll leave you alone now. Whenever you want to start, just say 'ready' into the microphone."

"Yes, sir."

The man squeezed his shoulder, and left.

Dickie said, "Ready."

Lights appeared on the machine, and something inside whirred. A voice said:

"Complete this sequence. One, four, seven, ten . . ."

Mr. and Mrs. Jordan were in the living room, not speaking, not even speculating.

It was almost four o'clock when the telephone rang. The woman tried to reach it first, but her husband was quicker.

"Mr. Jordan?"

The voice was cool; a brisk, official voice.

"Yes, speaking."

"This is the Government Educational Service. Your son, Richard M. Jordan, Classification 600-115, has completed the Government examination. We regret to inform you that his intelligence quotient is higher than the Government regulation, according to Rule 84, Section 5, of the New Code."

Across the room, the woman cried out, knowing nothing except the emotion she read on her husband's face.

"You may tell us by telephone," the voice went on, "whether you wish his body buried by the Government or would you prefer a private burial place? The fee for Government burial is ten dollars."

Recall

1. Dickie's twelfth birthday is nearly ruined by what (a) he knows (b) his parents know (c) only the government knows.

2. "Thousands of children take this test every day. The Government wants to know how smart you are, Dickie. That's all there is to it." Of these three sentences, the one that is untrue is (a) the first (b) the second (c) the third.

3. The examination is actually given by a (a) computing machine (b) uniformed attendant (c) person on the telephone.

4. When taking the test Dickie (a) gets ill with a fever (b) tells more than he should (c) forgets everything he knew.

5. At the end of the story, Dickie is to be (a) given a prize (b) sent to a special school (c) killed.

Infer

6. Early in the story, the father tells Dickie that the sun is five thousand miles away. The father probably (a) thinks this is the true figure (b) is giving wrong information on purpose (c) has absolutely no idea how far away the sun is.

7. With regard to what "the Government" is doing, Mr. and Mrs. Jordan seem to (a) be very approving and enthusiastic (b) simply accept it (c) oppose and fight it.

8. The "stuff to drink" was probably to (a) make Dickie sleepy (b) make sure Dickie didn't give wrong answers on purpose (c) reward Dickie for right answers.

9. Can you complete the sequence given in the story? One, four, seven, ten, (a) twelve (b) thirteen (c) fourteen.

10. The story presents a frightening way for "the Government" to bring about the old ideal of (a) equality (b) freedom (c) individual rights.

Vocabulary Review

Write on your paper the term in *italics* that belongs in each blank. Use each term only once.

attendant   *multi-dialed*
computing   *sequence*
consistency   *speculate*

1. Mom's paycheck is figured out by a huge ———— machine.
2. The four candidates for class president argued about the ———— in which they'd give their speeches.
3. Most movie theaters have a(n) ———— who takes tickets.
4. S.A.E. 30 motor oil has a thicker ———— than S.A.E. 20 oil.
5. I take every day as it comes along and never ———— about the future.
6. A word beginning with a prefix meaning "many" is ————.

Critical Thinking

1. Why does the father first tell Dickie to read comic books and then fail to answer his questions properly?

2. Why is the "truth drug" necessary for the examination?

3. Explain as clearly as possible what "the Government" in the story is trying to do.

4. Many books and stories have been written on horrors of "the Government" of the future. What kind of a government do the Jordans live under? Could such a government ever rule the United States? Explain your answer.

5. So-called intelligence tests used to be given regularly to all young people. Many schools no longer use them. What's wrong with thinking that a score on a short test can really indicate a person's intelligence?

The King of the Beasts

Philip José Farmer

Did you ever go to the zoo and see a real live dinosaur? Of course not. The last dinosaur on earth died millions of years ago. Scientists know no way of bringing the dinosaur back to life.

In fact, no animal that entirely disappeared from the earth has ever been brought back. But who knows what will happen in the future? Wouldn't it be wonderful to go to a zoo and see every living thing that ever existed?

The story that follows imagines just such a future. "The King of the Beasts" is a tricky two-page treat. It's set in the future, but it points at the now. It deals with life, but it shocks us with death. It's short in length, but long on meaning. Read it carefully.

Vocabulary Preview

DISTINGUISHED (dis TING gwisht) excellent;
well-known; worthy of respect
  • The school always gets a *distinguished*
  speaker for graduation.
DODO (DOE doe) a large, flightless bird that
no longer exists
  • The last *dodo* lived 300 years ago.
EMBRYO (EM bree o) an animal before the
stage of birth
  • The biologist removed an *embryo* from
  the body of the female rabbit.
EXTINCT (ek STINKT) no longer living on
earth
  • The dodo has been *extinct* for about 300
  years.
RESTORE (rih STORE) to bring back to
original condition
  • I'd like to *restore* a very old car.
STRUT (STRUT) to walk or march with a stiff,
self-important step
  • The rooster *strutted* around as if he
  owned the barnyard.
TRANSLATE (TRANZ late) to put in the words
of another language
  • The Bible has been *translated* into
  almost every language.

THE BIOLOGIST WAS SHOWING THE DISTIN-
guished visitor through the zoo and laboratory.

"Our budget," she said, "is too small to bring back all
known extinct animals. So we bring to life only the beautiful
ones that were so cruelly killed off. I'm trying, as it were, to
make up for all the unkind and stupid things that were done
long ago. You might say that humans struck God in the face
every time they wiped out a kind of animal that might have
lived on."

She paused, and they looked across the ponds and fields.
The zebra turned and galloped, delight and sun flashing off
its back. The sea otter poked its humorous whiskers from the
water. The gorilla peered from behind a fence. Passenger
pigeons strutted. A rhinoceros trotted like a dainty battle-
ship. With gentle eyes a giraffe looked at them, then went on
eating leaves.

"There's the dodo. Not beautiful but very interesting.
And very helpless. Come. I'll show you how we bring these
extinct animals back to life."

In the great building, they passed between rows of tall
and wide tanks. They could see clearly through the windows
and through the jelly within.

"Those are African elephant embryos," said the biologist. "We plan to grow a large group of them, and then let
them go on the new government lands."

"You're really wonderful," said the distinguished visitor.
"You really love the animals, don't you?"

"I love all life."

157

"Tell me," said the visitor, "where do you learn just what these long-dead animals were like?"

"Mostly, skeletons and skins from the old museums. Ancient books and movies that we succeeded in translating and restoring. Ah, see those huge eggs? The chicks of the giant ostrich are growing inside them. These, almost ready to be taken from the tank, are baby tigers. They'll be dangerous when grown, but we'll keep them on government lands."

The visitor stopped before the last of the tanks.

"Just one?" he said. "What is it?"

"Poor little thing," said the biologist, now sad. "It will be so alone. But I shall give it all the love I have."

"Is it so dangerous?" said the visitor. "Worse than elephants, tigers and bears?"

"I had to get special permission to grow this one," said the biologist. Her voice shook.

The visitor stepped sharply back from the tank. She said, "Then it must be. . . . But you wouldn't dare!"

The biologist nodded.

"Yes. It's a human."

Recall

1. The biologist shows her visitor through the (a) zoo and laboratory (b) museum and gardens (c) fields and pastures.
2. The biologist believes that the killing off of so many kinds of animals was (a) a good thing (b) of no importance at all (c) unkind and stupid.
3. The biologist makes it very clear that she loves (a) only extinct animals (b) people more than animals (c) all life.

4. The biologist brings extinct animals to life (a) by thawing out animals frozen thousands of years (b) by creating eggs and embryos (c) by building real adult animals in her lab.
5. The word that usually means the same thing as the title of the story is (a) lion (b) tiger (c) elephant.

Infer

6. The story is supposed to happen (a) today (b) in the near future (c) in the distant future.
7. The biologist and her visitor are both (a) humans (b) dodos (c) creatures of a future world.
8. It comes as a surprise to us that many of the animals the biologist is bringing back to life are (a) alive today (b) now extinct (c) birds.
9. The "jelly" inside the tanks is probably (a) food for the embryos (b) embryos (c) water.
10. In the story, humans are seen in a bad light because they (a) never love anything (b) fight among themselves (c) kill off other kinds of life.

Vocabulary Review

Write on your paper the word in *italics* that belongs in each blank. Use each word only once.

distinguished	*extinct*	*strut*
dodo	*restore*	*translate*
embryo		

1. The —————— is a(n) —————— bird.
2. When the home run hit left her bat, Diane knew she could laugh her way around the bases and —————— across the plate.

3. A human —————— after the eighth week is also called a "fetus."

4. The very —————— scientist who discovers a cure for cancer is likely to be a biologist.

5. The Indians wanted to —————— their old village and to —————— their ancient stories into modern English.

Critical Thinking

1. "You might say that humans struck God in the face every time they wiped out a kind of animal that might have lived on." Why, exactly, does the biologist say this? If you have trouble, open a Bible to the very beginning and read *Genesis* 1:24-31.

2. What animal is usually called "king of the beasts"? How does the author change our thinking on this point? Do you think he's right? Explain.

3. In one sentence, what is the meaning of the story? What is the meaning in terms of things we can do in today's world?

4. The story mentions two birds that are extinct today: the dodo and the passenger pigeon. The first has been discussed in "Word Warm-up." But what does it mean when we call another person a "dodo"? Look the word up if you have to. Also look up *passenger pigeon.* It's an interesting bird with an interesting story.

Something Green

Fredric Brown

Ready for a space trip? Okay, join McGarry in
the story that follows. You've climbed into a small
spacer and blasted off. You've traveled far, far out
. . . past the planets Mars and Venus . . . past
Jupiter even . . . to a distant sun called Kruger.
Then—TROUBLE. You've made a crash landing
on Kruger III, one of the sun's planets. Now your
spacer's a wreck. You're stuck on a red and brown
planet far from Earth, and you're very homesick.
You dream of getting back to Earth, of meeting old
friends, of tasting Earth food, and more than
anything, of seeing "Something Green."

Vocabulary Preview

CRIMSON (KRIM zun) a bright purplish red
  • Alison's bad sunburn was nearly *crimson.*

DELUSION (dih LEW zhun) something imagined by the mind; something unreal
  • People who are not sane sometimes see *delusions* they take for real.

HORIZON (huh RI zun) the line where the earth seems to meet the sky
  • We watched the airplane till it disappeared over the *horizon.*

OCCASIONAL (uh KAY zhun ul) happening from time to time
  • My health is excellent except for an *occasional* cold.

PLAIN (PLANE) a large flat area of ground
  • The cowboys rode across the *plain.*

REASONABLY (REE zun uh blee) fairly; within reasonable limits
  • Monique gets *reasonably* good marks in school.

THE BIG SUN WAS CRIMSON IN A VIOLET sky. At the edge of the brown plain, dotted with brown bushes, lay the red jungle.

McGarry walked toward it. It was tough work and dangerous work, searching in those red jungles, but it had to be done. And he'd searched a thousand of them; this was just one more.

He said, "Here we go, Dorothy. All set?"

The little five-limbed creature that rested on his shoulder didn't answer, but then it never did. It couldn't talk, but it was something to talk to. It was company. In size and weight it felt amazingly like a hand resting on his shoulder.

He'd had Dorothy for—how long? At a guess, four years. He'd been here about five, as nearly as he could reckon it, and it had been about a year before he'd found her. Anyway, he assumed that Dorothy was a "she," if for no better reason than the way she rested on his shoulder, like a woman's hand.

"Dorothy," he said, "reckon we'd better get ready for trouble. Might be lions or tigers in there."

He unbuckled his sol-gun and let his hand rest on it, ready to draw it quickly. For the thousandth time, at least, he thanked his lucky stars that the weapon he'd managed to save from the wreck of his spacer had been a sol-gun, the one and only weapon that worked practically forever. A sol-gun soaked up energy. And, when you pulled the trigger, it dished it out. With any weapon but a sol-gun he'd never have lasted even one year on Kruger III.

163

Yes, even before he quite reached the edge of the red jungle, he saw a lion. Nothing like any lion ever seen on Earth, of course. This one was bright magenta,[1] just enough different in color from the purplish bushes it crouched behind so he could see it. It had eight legs, all as strong as an elephant's trunk, and a head with a beak like a large bird's.

McGarry called it a lion. He had as much right to call it that as anything else, because it had never been named. Or if it had, the namer had never returned to Earth to report on the plants and animals of Kruger III. Only one spacer had ever landed here before McGarry's, as far as the records showed, and it had never taken off again. He was looking for it now; he'd been looking for it for the five years he'd been here.

If he found it, it might—just barely might—contain some of the transistors which had been destroyed in the crash-landing of his own spacer. And if it contained enough of them, he could get back to Earth.

He stopped ten steps short of the edge of the red jungle and aimed the sol-gun at the bushes behind which the lion crouched. He pulled the trigger and there was a bright green flash, brief but beautiful—oh, so beautiful—and the bushes weren't there any more, and neither was the lion.

McGarry chuckled softly. "Did you see that, Dorothy? That was *green,* the one color you don't have on this bloody red planet of yours. The most beautiful color in the universe, Dorothy. *Green!* And I know where there's a world that's mostly green, and we're going to get there, you and I. Sure we are. It's the world I came from, and it's the most beautiful place there is, Dorothy. You'll love it."

He turned and looked back over the brown plain with brown bushes, the violet sky above, the crimson sun. The crimson sun Kruger, which never set on the day side of this planet, one side of which always faced it as one side of Earth's moon always faces Earth.

[1] magenta *(muh JEN tuh)—reddish purple.*

No day and night—unless one passed the shadow line into the night side, which was too cold for life. No seasons. A steady, never-changing temperature, no wind, no storms.

He thought for the thousandth, or the millionth, time that it wouldn't be a bad planet to live on, if only it were green like Earth, if only there was something green upon it besides the occasional flash of his sol-gun. It had air you could breathe and a temperature ranging from about forty near the shadow line to about ninety at the point directly under the red sun, where its rays were straight down instead of slanting. Plenty of food, and he'd learned long ago which plants and animals were good to eat and which made him ill. Nothing he'd ever tried was really poisonous.

Yes, a wonderful world. He'd even got used, by now, to being the only intelligent creature on it. Dorothy was helpful, there. Something to talk to, even if she didn't talk back.

Except—Oh, God—he wanted to see a *green* world again.

Earth, the only planet where green was the color, where plant life was based on chlorophyll.[2] Why, you could live years on any planet but Earth, anywhere, and never see green.

McGarry sighed. He'd been thinking to himself, but now he thought out loud, to Dorothy, continuing his thoughts without a break. It didn't matter to Dorothy. "Yes, Dorothy," he said, "it's the only planet worth living on—Earth! Green fields, grassy lawns, green trees. Dorothy, I'll never leave it again, once I get back there. I'll build me a shack out in the woods, in the middle of trees, but not trees so thick that the grass doesn't grow under them. *Green* grass. And I'll paint the shack green, Dorothy. We've even got green paints back on Earth."

He sighed and looked at the red jungle ahead of him.

"What's that you asked, Dorothy?" She hadn't asked

[2] chlorophyll (KLOR uh fil)—the green substance in growing plants.

165

anything, but it was a game to pretend that she talked back, a game to keep him sane. "Will I get married when I get back? Is that what you asked?"

He thought about it. "Well, it's like this, Dorothy. Maybe and maybe not. You were named after a woman back on Earth, you know. A woman I was going to marry. But five years is a long time, Dorothy. I've been reported missing and am probably thought dead. I doubt if she's waited this long. If she has, well, I'll marry her, Dorothy.

"Did you ask, what if she hasn't? Well, I don't know. Let's not worry about that till I get back, huh? Of course, if I could find a woman who was *green,* or even one with green hair, I'd love her to pieces. But on Earth almost everything is green *except* the woman."

He chuckled at that and, sol-gun ready, went on into the jungle, the red jungle that had nothing green except the occasional flash of his sol-gun.

Maybe that, he thought, had been the one thing that, besides Dorothy's company, had kept him sane. A flash of green several times a day. Something green to remind him what the color *was.* To keep his eyes used to it, if he ever saw it again.

It turned out to be a small patch of jungle, as patches of jungle went on Kruger III. One of what seemed countless millions of such patches. And maybe it really was millions; Kruger III was larger than Jupiter. Actually it might take him more than a lifetime to cover it all. He knew that, but did not let himself think about it. No more than he let himself think that the other ship might have crashed on the dark side, the cold side. Or than he let himself doubt that, once he found the ship, he would find the transistors he needed to make his own spacer run again.

The patch of jungle was less than a mile wide, but he had to sleep once and eat several times before he had finished it.

He killed two more lions and one tiger. And when he finished it, he walked around it, marking each of the larger trees along the outer rim so he wouldn't repeat by searching this particular jungle again. The trees were soft; his pocketknife took off the red bark down to the pink wood as easily as it would have taken the skin off a potato.

Then out across the dull brown plain again, this time holding his sol-gun in the open to recharge it.

"Not that one, Dorothy. Maybe the next. The one over there near the horizon. Maybe it's there."

Violet sky, red sun, brown plain.

"The green gills of Earth, Dorothy. Oh, how you'll love them."

The brown never-ending plain.

The never-changing violet sky.

Was there a sound up there? There couldn't be. There never had been. But he looked up. And saw it.

A tiny black speck high in the violet, moving. *A spacer. It had to be a spacer. There were no birds on Kruger III. And birds don't have jets of fire behind them—*

He knew what to do; he'd thought of it a million times, how he could signal a spacer if one ever came in sight. He raised his sol-gun, aimed it straight into the violet air and pulled the trigger. It didn't make a big flash, from the distance of the spacer, but it made a *green* flash. If the pilot were only looking or if he would only look before he got out of sight, he couldn't miss a green flash on a world with no other green.

He pulled the trigger again.

And the pilot of the spacer *saw.* He cut and fired his jets three times—the standard answer to a signal of distress—and began to circle.

McGarry stood there trembling. So long a wait, and so sudden an end to it. He touched his left shoulder and touched the five-legged pet that felt to his fingers as well as to his naked shoulder so like a woman's hand.

"Dorothy," he said, "it's—" He ran out of words.

The spacer was closing in for a landing now. McGarry looked down at himself, suddenly ashamed of himself, as he would look to a rescuer. His body was naked except for the belt that held his gun and from which hung his knife and a few other tools. He was dirty and probably smelled, although he could not smell himself. And under the dirt his body looked thin and wasted, almost old, but that was due of course to his diet; a few months of proper food, Earth food, would take care of that.

Earth! The green hills of Earth!

He ran now, stumbling sometimes in his hurry, toward the point where the spacer was landing. He could see now that it was a one-man job, like his own had been. But that was all right; it could carry two in an emergency, at least as far as the nearest planet where he could get other transportation back to Earth. To the green hills, the green fields, the green valleys.

He prayed a little and swore a little as he ran. There were tears running down his cheeks.

He was there, waiting, as the door opened and a tall slender young man in the uniform of the Space Patrol stepped out.

"You'll take me back?" he shouted.

"Of course," said the young man calmly. "Been here long?"

"Five years!" McGarry knew that he was crying, but he couldn't stop.

"Good Lord!" said the young man. "I'm Lieutenant Archer. Of course I'll take you back, man, as soon as my jets cool enough for a takeoff. I'll take you as far as Carthage, on Aldebaran II, anyway; you can get a ship out of there for

168

anywhere. Need anything right away? Food? Water?"

McGarry shook his head. Food, water—What did such things matter now?

The green hills of Earth! He was going back to them. *That* was what mattered, and all that mattered. So long a wait, then so sudden an ending. He saw the violet sky swimming and then it suddenly went black as his knees gave way under him.

He was lying flat and the young man was holding something to his lips and he took a long drink of the fiery stuff it held. He sat up and felt better. He looked to make sure the spacer was still there; it was, and he felt wonderful.

The young man said, "Buck up, old-timer; we'll be off in half an hour. You'll be in Carthage in six hours. Want to talk, till you get your feet under you again? Want to tell me all about it, everything that's happened?"

They sat in the shadow of a brown bush, and McGarry told him about it, everything about it. The five-year search for the other ship he'd read had crashed on the planet and which might have the parts he needed to repair his own ship. The long search. About Dorothy, perched on his shoulder, and how she'd been something to talk to.

But somehow, the face of Lieutenant Archer was changing as McGarry talked. It grew even more serious, even more kind.

"Old-timer," Archer asked gently, "what year was it when you came here?"

McGarry saw it coming. How can you keep track of time on a planet whose sun and seasons are unchanging? A planet where it's always day, always summer—

He said flatly, "I came here in twenty-two forty-two. How much am I off, Lieutenant? How old am I—instead of thirty, as I've thought?"

"It's twenty-two seventy-two, McGarry. You came here

169

thirty years ago. You're fifty-five. But don't let that worry you too much. Medical science has advanced. You still have a long time to live."

McGarry said it softly. "Fifty-five. *Thirty years.*"

The lieutenant looked at him with pity. He said, "Old-timer, do you want it all in a lump, all the rest of the bad news? There are several items of it. I'm no psychologist but I think maybe it's best for you to take it now, all at once, while you can still balance against it the fact that you're going back. Can you take it, McGarry?"

There couldn't be anything worse than he'd learned already. The fact that thirty years of his life had already been wasted here. Sure, he could take the rest of whatever it was, as long as he was getting back to Earth, green Earth.

He stared at the violet sky, the red sun, the brown plain. He said, very quietly, "I can take it. Dish it out."

"You've done wonderfully for thirty years, McGarry. You can thank God for the fact that you believed Marley's spacer crashed on Kruger III; it was Kruger IV. You'd have never found it here, but the search, as you say, kept you—reasonably sane." He paused a moment. His voice was gentle when he spoke again. "There isn't anything on your shoulder, McGarry. This Dorothy is just something in your imagination. But don't worry about it; that particular delusion has probably kept you from cracking up completely."

McGarry put up his hand. It touched his shoulder. Nothing else.

Archer said, "My God, man, it's marvelous that you're *otherwise* okay. Thirty years alone; it's almost a miracle. And if your one delusion continues, now that I've told you it *is* a delusion, a psychiatrist back at Carthage or on Mars can fix you up in a jiffy."

McGarry said dully, "It doesn't continue. It isn't there now. I—I'm not even sure, Lieutenant, that I ever did really believe in Dorothy. I think I made her up on purpose, to talk to, so I'd remain sane except for that. She was—she was like a woman's hand, Lieutenant. Or did I tell you that?"

"You told me. Want the rest of it now, McGarry?"

McGarry stared at him. "The rest of it? What rest can there be? I'm fifty-five instead of thirty. I've spent thirty years, since I was twenty-five, hunting for a spacer I'd never have found, since it's on another planet. I've been crazy—in one way, but only one—most of that time. But none of that matters now that I can go back to Earth."

Lieutenant Archer was shaking his head slowly. "Not back to Earth, old-timer. To Mars if you wish, the beautiful brown and yellow hills of Mars. Or, if you don't mind heat, to purple Venus. But not to Earth, McGarry. Nobody lives there any more."

"Earth is—gone? I don't—"

"Not gone, McGarry It's there. But it's black and life-less, a burned out planet. The war with the Arcturians, twenty years ago. They struck first, and got Earth. We got *them,* we won, we wiped them out, but Earth was gone before we started. I'm sorry, but you'll have to settle for somewhere else."

McGarry said, "No Earth." There was no feeling in his voice. No feeling at all.

Archer said, "That's the works, old-timer. But Mars isn't so bad. You'll get used to it. It's the center of things now, and there are three billion humans on it. You'll miss the green of Earth, sure, but it's not so bad."

McGarry said, "No Earth." There was no feeling in his voice. No feeling at all.

Archer nodded. "Glad you can take it that way, old-timer. It must be rather a shock. Well, I guess we can get going. The tubes ought to have cooled enough by now. I'll check and make sure."

171

He stood up and started toward the little spacer.

McGarry's sol-gun came out. McGarry shot him, and Lieutenant Archer wasn't there any more. McGarry stood up and walked to the little spacer. He aimed the sol-gun at it and pulled the trigger. Part of the spacer was gone. Half a dozen shots and it was completely gone. Little atoms that had been the spacer and little atoms that had been Lieutenant Archer of the Space Patrol may have danced in the air, but they couldn't be seen.

McGarry put the gun back on his belt and started walking toward the red patch of jungle near the horizon.

He put his hand up to his shoulder and touched Dorothy and she was there, as she'd been there now for four of the five years he'd been on Kruger III. She felt, to his fingers and to his bare shoulder, like a woman's hand.

He said, "Don't worry, Dorothy, We'll find it. Maybe this next jungle is the right one. And when we find it—"

He was near the edge of the jungle now, the red jungle, and a tiger came running out to meet him and eat him. A tiger with six legs and a head like a barrel. McGarry aimed his sol-gun and pulled the trigger, and there was a bright green flash, brief but beautiful—oh, so beautiful—and the tiger wasn't there any more.

McGarry chuckled softly. "Did you see that, Dorothy? That was *green,* the color there isn't much of on any planet but the one we're going to. The only green planet in the system, and it's the one I came from. You'll love it."

She said, "I know I will, Mac." Her low throaty voice was completely familiar to him, as familiar as his own; she'd always answered him. He reached up his hand and touched her as she rested on his naked shoulder. She felt like a woman's hand.

He turned and looked back over the brown plain dotted with brown bushes, the violet sky above, the crimson sun.

He laughed at it. Not a mad laugh, a gentle one. It didn't matter because soon now he'd find the spacer so he could go back to Earth.

To the green hills, the green fields, the green valleys. Once more he patted the hand upon his shoulder and spoke to it, listened to its answer.

Then, gun at ready, he entered the red jungle.

Recall

1. For years, McGarry has searched the red jungles for (a) lions and tigers (b) food (c) a wrecked spacer.
2. To get back to Earth, McGarry needs (a) a sol-gun (b) transistors (c) something green.
3. The only green on Kruger III is (a) Dorothy (b) the trees (c) the flash of the sol-gun.
4. At the beginning of the story, McGarry thinks he's been on Kruger III for about (a) a year (b) five years (c) thirty years.
5. Several times in the story, the sky is described as (a) crimson (b) blue (c) violet.
6. Dorothy has been named for (a) a woman on Earth (b) McGarry's spacer (c) McGarry's mother.
7. When he meets Lieutenant Archer, McGarry is most excited about (a) food (b) water (c) returning to Earth.
8. McGarry learns from Archer that (a) he is really on Mars (b) Earth has been destroyed (c) Dorothy is green.

9. McGarry also learns that the other spacer had crashed (a) on the dark side of Kruger III (b) in one of the red jungles (c) on Kruger IV.

10. McGarry's reaction to Archer's statements is to (a) shoot him (b) argue about Dorothy (c) be even more eager to leave.

11. The story ends with McGarry and Dorothy (a) searching the wreck of Archer's spacer (b) about to return to Earth (c) searching the jungles again.

12. The ending of the story is much like the beginning, except that in the end (a) it is evening instead of morning (b) McGarry's chances are better (c) Dorothy talks.

Infer

13. On Kruger III, McGarry probably *never* saw a (a) river (b) strange animal (c) snowstorm.

14. McGarry probably created Dorothy to (a) protect him from the animals (b) keep him company (c) find food.

15. When he talks about McGarry's age, Dorothy, and the planet Earth, Lieutenant Archer is probably (a) trying to be helpful (b) just kidding McGarry (c) lying to protect McGarry's feelings.

16. McGarry destroys Archer's spacer because (a) it offers no true escape (b) it contains no transistors (c) he doesn't want Archer to leave.

17. At the end of the story, McGarry is (a) married to Dorothy (b) likely to find the spacer (c) insane.

18. At the end of the story, McGarry still has (a) his youth (b) hope (c) a real chance.

174

19. The story shows that people (a) are afraid to travel to other planets (b) sometimes lie to each other (c) sometimes cannot accept the truth.

Vocabulary Review

1. A *reasonably* good mark on a test would be a (a) 40 (b) 85 (c) 99.
2. The *plain* stretched out to the far *horizon.* In other words the (a) airplane vanished into the sky (b) ground went up suddenly (c) flat area continued till it met the distant sky.
3. *Crimson* is a bright color between (a) blue and green (b) green and purple (c) purple and red.
4. Some people have *occasional delusions.* In other words, they (a) sometimes see things that aren't really there (b) frequently get angry (c) have an occupational disease.

Critical Thinking

1. Why was it always daytime on Kruger III? Why were there no seasons? Drawing a picture will help you explain.
2. Explain why McGarry had probably created Dorothy. Then explain why he admitted to Lieutenant Archer that she didn't exist. Finally, explain why she existed once more for McGarry at the end of the story.

3. What does Dorothy's talking at the end of the story tell us about McGarry?

4. In spite of the fact that McGarry is in a strange place in a strange time, and does some of the strangest things, he seems—strangely—believable. Did you have any trouble believing in him as a human character? If so, explain.

5. How did you feel toward McGarry at the end of the story? Explain in detail.

The Gift

Ray Bradbury

How many different kinds of science fiction
stories have you read so far in this book? Well,
there's the scary sci-fi story (remember
"Examination Day"?). There's also the funny sci-
fi story ("In Our Block"), the shocking sci-fi story
("The King of the Beasts"), and even the "true"
sci-fi story ("The Flatwoods Monster"). Now it's
time for something new: the beautiful sci-fi story.
And the beautiful sci-fi story is the specialty of
author Ray Bradbury, probably the best sci-fi
writer of our time.

"The Gift" is a Christmas story of the future.
It starts in a rocket port (like an airport, but a
terminal for rockets, not airplanes). Climb aboard,
relax, and wait for a truly beautiful present.

Vocabulary Preview

ABANDONED (uh BAN dund) given up; left alone
  • An *abandoned* old car has been sitting on our street for months.
CLASH (KLASH) a loud collison or argument
  • Mom and I get along fine, but I have *clash* after *clash* with Dad.
CUSTOMS (KUS tumz) the inspection of baggage entering or leaving a country
  • The *customs* official made us empty our suitcase on a table.
DEPRIVED (dih PRIVD) to have something taken away from one
  • Seniors caught smoking will be *deprived* of their privileges.
DISMAYED (dis MAID) saddened; annoyed
  • The teacher was *dismayed* at our poor marks on the test.
EXCEED (ek SEED) to go beyond certain limits
  • Dan admitted that the speed of his car did *exceed* the limit.

Tomorrow would be christmas, and even while the three of them rode to the rocket port the mother and father were worried. It was the boy's first flight into space, his very first time in a rocket, and they wanted everything to be perfect. So when, at the customs table, they were forced to leave behind his gift which exceeded the weight limit by no more than a few ounces and the little tree with the lovely white candles, they felt themselves deprived of the season and their love.

The boy was waiting for them in the Terminal room. Walking toward him, after their unsuccessful clash with the Interplanetary officials, the mother and father whispered to each other.

"What shall we do?"

"Nothing, nothing. What *can* we do?"

"Silly rules!"

"And he so wanted the tree!"

The siren gave a great howl and people pressed forward into the Mars Rocket. The mother and father walked at the very last, their small pale son between them, silent.

"I'll think of something," said the father.

"What . . . ?" asked the boy.

And the rocket took off and they were flung headlong into dark space.

The rocket moved and left fire behind and left Earth behind on which the date was December 24, 2052, heading out into a place where there was no time at all, no month, no year, no hour. They slept away the rest of the first "day." Near midnight, by their Earth-time New York watches, the boy awoke and said, "I want to go look out the porthole."

179

There was only one port, a "window" of immensely thick glass of some size, up on the next deck.

"Not quite yet," said the father. "I'll take you up later."

"I want to see where we are and where we're going."

"I want you to wait for a reason," said the father.

He had been lying awake, turning this way and that, thinking of the abandoned gift, the problem of the season, the lost tree and the white candles. And at last, sitting up, no more than five minutes ago, he believed he had found a plan. He need only carry it out and this journey would be fine and joyous indeed.

"Son," he said, "in exactly one half hour it will be Christmas."

"Oh," said the mother, dismayed that he had mentioned it. Somehow she had rather hoped that the boy would forget.

The boy's face grew feverish and his lips trembled. "I know, I know. Will I get a present, will I? Will I have a tree? You promised—"

"Yes, yes, all that, and more," said the father.

The mother started. "But—"

"I mean it," said the father. "I really mean it. All and more, much more. Excuse me, now. I'll be back."

He left them for about twenty minutes. When he came back he was smiling. "Almost time."

"Can I hold your watch?" asked the boy, and the watch was handed over and he held it ticking in his fingers as the rest of the hour drifted by in fire and silence and unfelt motion.

"It's Christmas *now!* Christmas! Where's my present?"

"Here we go," said the father and took his boy by the shoulder and led him from the room, down the hall, up a rampway, his wife following.

"I don't understand," she kept saying.

"You will. Here we are," said the father.

They had stopped at the closed door of a large cabin. The father tapped three times and then twice in a code. The door opened and the light in the cabin went out and there was a whisper of voices.

"Go on in, son," said the father.

"It's dark."

"I'll hold your hand. Come on, Mama."

They stepped into the room and the door shut, and the room was very dark indeed. And before them loomed a great glass eye, the porthole, a window four feet high and six feet wide, from which they could look out into space.

The boy gasped.

Behind him, the father and the mother gasped with him, and then in the dark room some people began to sing.

"Merry Christmas, son," said the father.

And the voices in the room sang the old, the familiar carols, and the boy moved forward slowly until his face was pressed against the cool glass of the port. And he stood there for a long long time, just looking out into space and the deep night at the burning and the burning of ten billion billion white and lovely candles. . . .

Recall

1. In the beginning of the story, the family is saddened because (a) they are being forced to leave Earth (b) the whole family cannot go on the trip (c) they've had to leave both tree and present behind.
2. The mother and father argue with (a) each other (b) the officials (c) the boy.

3. The idea for the "gift" of the story's title is (a) the boy's (b) the father's (c) the mother's.
4. The gift has to be given in the large cabin because (a) the boy's school friends are there (b) that's where the window is (c) only the large room is big enough to hold it.
5. The sound in the reader's ears at the end of the story is (a) Santa's "Ho! Ho!" through space (b) the hiss of rocket jets (c) Christmas carols.

Infer

6. The boy in the story seems to be about (a) two (b) six (c) fifteen.
7. In space there is "no time at all" because (a) regularly occuring natural events have been left behind on Earth (b) watches and clocks do not work in space (c) in space everything happens at once.
8. The father knocks on the door of the large cabin in a code because (a) he doesn't want everyone inside to know what's happening (b) codes are common for space communication (c) he has arranged the family's visit there with the people inside.
9. The "candles" in the last sentence of the story are really (a) stars (b) rockets (c) Christmas tree lights.

Vocabulary Review

1. Marianne was *dismayed* at the news. In other words, she was (a) surprised (b) saddened (c) pleased.

2. In a foreign country, the *customs* officer is most likely to (a) conduct a guided tour (b) sell tickets (c) inspect baggage.

3. A person who feels *deprived* wants (a) something back (b) to make others happy (c) absolutely nothing.

4. A person who feels *abandoned* wants (a) more money (b) love and friendship (c) adventure and excitement.

5. The *clash* had *exceeded* the rules of good behavior. In other words people were (a) having a good time (b) arguing in an unruly fashion (c) being sneaky.

Critical Thinking

1. Ray Bradbury's world of 2052 seems to be quite different from our world. For instance, people think of a rocket to Mars in much the same way that we might think of an airplane flight to a faraway city. But in some ways Bradbury's world is very much like our world. Try to think of at least two or three similarities. Do you think Bradbury is right in assuming that these things will go on into the future? Explain.

2. The little boy's Christmas gift was hardly what you'd see looking up into the sky on a clear night. The heavens seen from a point in outer space look quite different from the sky we see.

Use a reference book to find out what these differences are and what accounts for them.

3. Many science fiction stories view the distant future as a time of trouble and horrors we can only begin to imagine. But the world of "The Gift" is a *good* world. What's your guess?

Will people in the distant future be happier than we are? Sadder? About the same? Explain your answer.

4. "The Gift" comes from *R is for Rocket,* a book of Ray Bradbury's stories selected especially for young people. Two other popular books by Bradbury are *The Martian Cronicles* and *Dandelion Wine.* Read at least one other story by Bradbury and report on it.

The One Who Waits

Ray Bradbury

*Our exploration of space may just be
beginning. In 1969 we sent people to the moon for
the first time. Seven years later, in 1976, we sent a
rocket to explore Mars. No people made that trip,
but the rocket did sent back messages about the
soil and air, as well as sharp photographs of the
planet's surface.*

*What will happen when humans finally do
land on Mars? First, perhaps, they'll climb out of
their rocket and claim all the land on Mars for the
planet Earth. "We proclaim that all Martian
territory now belongs to Earth," they might say.
And then what? Ray Bradbury has a soul-stirring
idea.*

Vocabulary Preview

ALIEN (A lee un) foreign; in sci-fi stories, from another planet
- Will Earth ever be invaded by *alien* creatures from outer space?

CLAMOR (KLAM ur) to shout or cry in a very excited way
- In case of fire, stay calm, follow instructions, and don't *clamor.*

HOVER (HUV ur) to float in the air
- During the football game a helicopter *hovered* over the field.

PARCHED (PARCHT) dried up
- Boy, did that water taste good to my *parched* mouth!

PLEAD (PLEED) to beg; to ask and ask
- Small children often *plead* for candy or ice cream.

SEIZURE (SEE zhur) a fit; a period when the body cannot be controlled
- Mr. Newman's heart attack started with a sudden *seizure.*

VAPOR (VA pur) cloudy or damp air; mist
- The kitchen was thick with *vapor* from the stove.

I LIVE IN A WELL. I LIVE LIKE SMOKE IN THE well. Like vapor in a stone throat. I don't move. I don't do anything but wait. Overhead I see the cold stars of night and morning, and I see the sun. And sometimes I sing old songs of this world when it was young. How can I tell you what I am when I don't know? I cannot. I am simply waiting. I am mist and moonlight and memory. I am sad and I am old. Sometimes I fall like rain into the well. Spider webs are startled into forming where my rain falls fast, on the water surface. I wait in cool silence and there will be a day when I no longer wait.

Now it is morning. I hear a great thunder. I smell fire from a distance. I hear a metal crashing. I wait. I listen.

Voices. Far away.

"All right!"

One voice. An alien voice. An alien tongue[1] I cannot know. No word is familiar. I listen.

"Send the men out!"

A crunching in crystal sands.

"Mars! So this is it!"

"Where's the flag?"

"Here, sir."

"Good, good."

The sun is high in the blue sky and its golden rays fill the well and I hang like a flower pollen,[2] invisible and misting in the warm light.

Voices.

"In the name of the Government of Earth, I proclaim this

---

[1] tongue (TUNG)—used here to mean "language."
[2] pollen (POL un)—the fine powder that forms in the center of flowers.

to be the Martian Territory, to be equally divided among the member nations."

What are they saying? I turn in the sun, like a wheel, invisible and lazy, golden and tireless.

"What's over here?"

"A well!"

"No!"

"Come on. Yes!"

The approach of warmth. Three objects bend over the well mouth, and my coolness rises to the objects.

"Great!"

"Think it's good water?"

"We'll see."

"Someone get a lab test bottle and a dropline."[3]

"I will!"

A sound of running. The return.

"Here we are."

I wait.

"Let it down. Easy."

Glass shines, above, coming down on a slow line.

The water ripples softly as the glass touches and fills. I rise in the warm air toward the well mouth.

"Here we are. You want to test this water, Regent?"

"Let's have it."

"What a beautiful well. Look at that construction. How old you think it is?"

"God knows. When we landed in that other town yesterday Smith said there hasn't been life on Mars in ten thousand years."

"Imagine."

"How is it, Regent? The water."

"Pure as silver. Have a glass."

[3] dropline (DROP line)—*a thin rope used to lower something, here the laboratory test bottle into the well.*

The sound of water in the hot sunlight. Now I hover like a dust, a cinnamon,[4] upon the soft wind.

"What's the matter, Jones?"

"I don't know. Got a terrible headache. All of a sudden."

"Did you drink the water yet?"

"No, I haven't. It's not that. I was just bending over the well and all of a sudden my head split. I feel better now."

Now I know who I am.

My name is Stephen Leonard Jones and I am twenty-five years old and I have just come in a rocket from a planet called Earth and I am standing with my good friends Regent and Shaw by an old well on the planet Mars.

I look down at my golden fingers, tan and strong. I look at my long legs and at my silver uniform and at my friends.

"What's wrong, Jones?" they say.

"Nothing," I say, looking at them. "Nothing at all."

The food is good. It has been ten thousand years since food. It touches the tongue in a fine way and the wine with the food is warming. I listen to the sound of voices. I make words that I do not understand but somehow understand. I test the air.

"What's the matter. Jones?"

I tilt this head of mine and rest my hands holding the silver utensils of eating. I feel everything.

"What do you mean?" this voice, this new thing of mine, says.

"You keep breathing funny. Coughing," says the other man.

I pronounce exactly. "Maybe a little cold coming on."

"Check with the doc later."

I nod my head and it is good to nod. It is good to do several things after ten thousand years. It is good to breathe the air and it is good to feel the sun in the flesh deep and

[4] cinnamon (SIN uh mun)—a powdered spice used in cooking.

189

going deeper and it is good to feel the structure of ivory,[5] the fine skeleton hidden in the warming flesh, and it is good to hear sounds much clearer and more immediate than they were in the stone deepness of a well. I sit enchanted.

"Come out of it, Jones. Snap to it. We got to move!"

"Yes," I say, hypnotized[6] with the way the word forms like water on the tongue and falls with slow beauty out into the air.

I walk and it is good walking. I stand high and it is a long way to the ground when I look down from my eyes and my head. It is like living on a fine cliff and being happy there.

Regent stands by the stone well, looking down. The others have gone murmuring to the silver ship from which they came.

I feel the fingers of my hand and the smile of my mouth.

"It is deep," I say.

"Yes."

"It is called a Soul Well."

Regent raises his head and looks at me. "How do you know that?"

"Doesn't it look like one?"

"I never heard of a Soul Well."

"A place where waiting things, things that once had flesh, wait and wait," I say, touching his arm.

The sand is fire and the ship is silver fire in the hotness of the day and the heat is good to feel. The sound of my feet in the hard sand. I listen. The sound of the wind and the sun burning the valleys. I smell the smell of the rocket boiling in the noon. I stand below the port.

"Where's Regent?" someone says.

"I saw him by the well," I reply.

One of them runs toward the well. I am beginning to

---

[5] structure of ivory—*something made of bone, here the skeleton.*
[6] hypnotized *(HIP nuh tized)—cast under a spell; in a trance.*

tremble. A fine shivering tremble, hidden deep, but becoming very strong. And for the first time I hear it, as if it too were hidden in a well. A voice calling deep within me, tiny and afraid. And the voice cries, *Let me go, let me go,* and there is a feeling as if something is trying to get free, a pounding of labyrinthine[7] doors, a rushing down dark corridors and up passages, echoing and screaming.

"Regent's in the well!"

The men are running, all five of them. I run with them but now I am sick and the trembling is violent.

"He must have fallen. Jones, you were here with him. Did you see? Jones? Well, speak up, man."

"What's wrong, Jones?"

I fall to my knees, the trembling is so bad.

"He's sick. Here, help me with him."

"The sun."

"No, not the sun," I murmur.

They stretch me out and the seizures come and go like earthquakes and the deep hidden voice in me cries, *This is Jones, this is me, that's not him, that's not him, don't believe him, let me out, let me out!* And I look up at the bent figures and my eyelids flicker. They touch my wrists.

"His heart is acting up."

I close my eyes. The screaming stops. The shivering ceases.

I rise, as in a cool well, released.

"He's dead," says someone.

"Jones is dead."

"From what?"

"Shock, it looks like."

"What kind of shock?" I say, and my name is Sessions and my lips move crisply, and I am the captain of these men. I stand among them and I am looking down at a body which

[7]labyrinthine *(lab uh RIN thin)—having to do with a labyrinth (LAB uh rinth) or maze, a place through which it is hard to find one's way.*

lies cooling on the sands. I clap both hands to my head.

"Captain!"

"It's nothing," I say, crying out. "Just a headache. I'll be all right. There. There," I whisper. "It's all right now."

"We'd better get out of the sun, sir."

"Yes," I say, looking down at Jones. "We should never have come. Mars doesn't want us."

We carry the body back to the rocket with us, and a new voice is calling deep in me to be let out.

Help, help. Far down in the moist earthen-works[8] of the body. *Help, help!* in red fathoms, echoing and pleading.

The trembling starts much sooner this time. The control is less steady.

"Captain, you'd better get in out of the sun, you don't look too well, sir."

"Yes," I say. "Help," I say.

"What, sir?"

"I didn't say anything."

"You said 'Help,' sir."

"Did I, Matthews, did I?"

The body is laid out in the shadow of the rocket and the voice screams in the deep underwater catacombs[9] of bone and crimson tide. My hands jerk. My mouth splits and is parched. My nostrils fasten wide. My eyes roll. *Help, help, oh help, don't, don't, let me out, don't, don't.*

"Don't," I say.

"What, sir?"

"Never mind," I say. "I've got to get free," I say. I clap my hand to my mouth.

"How's that, sir?" cries Matthews.

"Get inside, all of you, go back to Earth!" I shout.

A gun is in my hand. I lift it.

"Don't, sir!"

[8] moist earthen-works—*the damp, earthly stuff of which the body is made.*
[9] catacombs (KAT uh komz)—*underground passages containing graves.*

192

An explosion. Shadows run. The screaming is cut off. There is a whistling sound of falling through space.

After ten thousand years, how good to die. How good to feel the sudden coolness, the relaxation. How good to be like a hand within a glove that stretches out and grows wonderfully cold in the hot sand. Oh, the quiet and the loveliness of gathering, darkening death. But one cannot linger on.

A crack, a snap.

"Good God, he's killed himself!" I cry, and open my eyes and there is the captain lying against the rocket, his skull split by a bullet, his eyes wide, his tongue protruding between his white teeth. Blood runs from his head. I bend to him and touch him. "The fool," I say. "Why did he do that?"

The men are horrified. They stand over the two dead men and turn their heads to see the Martian sands and the distant well where Regent lies lolling[10] in deep waters. A croaking comes out of their dry lips, a whimpering, a childish protest against this awful dream.

The men turn to me.

After a long while, one of them says. "That makes you captain, Matthews."

"I know," I say slowly.

"Only six of us left."

"Good God, it happened so quick!"

"I don't want to stay here, let's get out!"

The men clamor. I go to them and touch them now, with a confidence which almost sings in me. "Listen," I say, and touch their elbows or their arms or their hands.

We all fall silent.

We are one.

No, no, no, no, no, no! Inner voices crying, deep down and gone into prisons beneath exteriors.

We are looking at each other. We are Samuel Matthews and Raymond Moses and William Spaulding and Charles

[10] lolling (LOL ling)—*lying down in a still and limp manner.*

Evans and Forrest Cole and John Summers, and we say nothing but look upon each other and our white faces and shaking hands.

We turn, as one, and look at the well.

"Now," we say.

No, no, six voices scream, hidden and layered down and stored forever.

Our feet walk in the sand and it is as if a great hand with twelve fingers were moving across the hot sea bottom.

We bend to the well, looking down. From the cool depths six faces peer back up at us.

One by one we bend until our balance is gone, and one by one drop into the mouth and down through cool darkness into the cold waters.

The sun sets. The stars wheel upon the night sky. Far out, there is a wink of light. Another rocket coming, leaving red marks on space.

I live in a well. I live like smoke in a well. Like vapor in a stone throat. Overhead I see the cold stars of night and morning, and I see the sun. And sometimes I sing old songs of this world when it was young. How can I tell you what I am when even I don't know? I cannot.

I am simply waiting.

Recall

1. The narrator (the teller of the story) is usually (a) formless (b) visible only to other Martians (c) very tall and heavy.
2. The first act of the men from Earth is to (a) test the water in the well (b) eat a good meal (c) claim Mars for the planet Earth.
3. When the men first see the well, they are (a) frightened (b) delighted (c) angry.

4. The men test the water and report that it is (a) unsafe (b) salty but safe (c) good.

5. During the story, the narrator speaks (a) in several languages (b) in several voices (c) only once.

6. The narrator states that his first experiences "in the flesh" in ten thousand years (eating, breathing, walking, etc.) are (a) enjoyable (b) frightening (c) painful.

7. Stephen Leonard Jones, the first man to fall ill, (a) trys to save the others (b) dies of seizures and shock (c) runs away crying.

8. Captain Sessions, who falls ill after Jones, (a) pushes Regent into the well when no one is looking(b) is saved by the Martian (c) kills himself.

9. Toward the end of the story, the six men who are left (a) escape in the rocket (b) kill each other (c) die together.

10. The very end of the story shows that the narrator (a) has learned a lot from his experience (b) is much like he was in the beginning (c) is eager to go to Earth.

Infer

11. At the time this story occurs there seems to be (a) war among the nations on Earth (b) cooperation on Earth (c) no one left alive on Earth.

12. The narrator can best be described as (a) a soul or spirit who lives in the well (b) a Martian soldier who hides in the well (c) the wisest man in the universe.

13. The narrator is able to (a) grow young or old at will (b) feel and think (c) walk, fly, and swim.

14. The well in the story is supposed to (a) lead to an underground city (b) be a doorway to a time machine (c) be at least ten thousand years old.

15. Stephen Leonard Jones, the first man to fall ill, has (a) drunk water from the well (b) been in the sun too long (c) had his body taken over by the narrator.

16. *"Let me go, let me go . . . let me out, let me out."* The speaker is (a) a human (b) a Martian (c) the one who waits.

17. Why does Captain Sessions shout, "Get inside, all of you, go back to Earth!" (a) It's the narrator whose voice really speaks these words. (b) He's begun to understand what is happening. (c) He wants to rule Mars himself.

18. The narrator seems to have (a) complete power over his own actions (b) little power over his own actions (c) power only when deep in the well.

19. As they approach their deaths, the men in the story seem to have (a) complete power over their own actions (b) little power over their own actions (c) power only when deep in the well.

20. It is clear from this story that the author, Ray Bradbury, (a) wants to tell what Mars is really like (b) has himself had his body taken over by outside forces (c) can write in a poetic manner.

Vocabulary Review

Write on your paper the word in *italics* that belongs in each blank. Use each word only once.

alien	*parched*	*seizure*
clamor	*plead*	*vapor*
hover		

1. It's hard to see clearly when there's too much —————— in the air.
2. Waiting for garbage, seagulls often —————— over large boats.
3. The home crowd began to —————— when the referee ruled against their team.
4. The referee could only —————— with them to be quiet.
5. Unless Don takes his pill every morning, he's likely to have a(n) —————— during the day.
6. Western Nebraska had had no rain for two months, and the grass looked ——————.
7. Who knows? There might be a(n) —————— sitting in this very classroom.

Critical Thinking

1. "The One Who Waits" is a confusing story for some readers. If you were confused, even for an instant, explain what confused you. If you experienced no confusion, explain what you think might confuse other readers. Refer to specific sentences and paragraphs.

2. The narrator of the story is a mysterious figure. Describe him as completely as you can. You should include his past history, his present purpose, and his possible future. Also include the powers that he seems—and doesn't seem—to have.

3. The last sentence of the first paragraph isn't easy to explain. How do *you* explain it?

4. Explain this sentence: "I make words that I do not understand but somehow understand."

197

5. Unlike most stories, "The One Who Waits" is written in the present tense. The verbs (words like *is, touches,* and *listens*) are those used for present time, not for past time (*was, touched, listened*). Explain why use of the present tense makes "The One Who Waits" a better story.

6. Several sentences in "The One Who Waits" seem to belong more to a poem than to a story. For instance, in the first paragraph we find "I am mist and moonlight and memory." Find at least five other sentences of similar beauty. If you can, explain why you find them "poetic."

7. Our rockets that explored Mars found nothing that resembled human life. Certainly, there were no little green men peering out from behind the rocks! Still, it's *barely* possible that events like those in the story could really happen someday. Explain why.

Finis

Frank Lillie Pollock

The first story in this book was called "Prolog," a word that means "introduction" or "beginning." So perhaps it's right that the last tale should be called "Finis," the French word for "end." This story as you may have guessed, deals with the end of the world, a subject that has always fascinated science fiction writers. Among hundreds of stories about the world's end, Pollack's "Finis," written in 1906, still stands as one of the best. The author has the power to make you see, smell, hear, and feel the death of a doomed city. Take a few deep breaths before you read this one. You'll see why later.

Vocabulary Preview

GLIMMER (GLIM er) a dim or flickering light
- The small candle produced only a *glimmer* of light.

SATELLITE (SAT ul ite) a moon; a small heavenly body that revolves around a larger one
- The moon is a *satellite* of the earth.

STAMPEDE (stam PEED) a sudden confused rush of a crowd of animals or people
- The circus tent caught fire, and three people were killed in the *stampede*.

THEORY (THEE uh ree) an idea, scientific law, or principle that is not yet proven
- The teacher had a *theory* that anyone could learn anything.

TIDAL WAVE (TIDE ul WAVE) an enormous, usually dangerous wave in the ocean
- The earthquake caused a *tidal wave* that nearly destroyed the city.

UNIVERSE (YEW nuh vers) everything that exists; the whole system of planets and stars
- Human beings have explored only a tiny part of the whole *universe*.

200

I'M GETTING TIRED," COMPLAINED DAVIS, looking out the window of the Science Building, "and sleepy. It's after eleven o'clock. This makes the fourth night I've sat up to see your new star. It'll be the last. Why, the thing was supposed to appear three weeks ago."

"Are *you* tired, Miss Wardour?" asked Eastwood and the girl glanced up with a quick blush, the glimmer of a smile, and a shake of the head.

Eastwood thought again that she certainly was painfully shy. She was almost as plain as she was shy. Though her hair had an unusual beauty of its own, fine as silk and colored like palest flame.

Probably she had brains; Eastwood had seen her reading some very "deep" books. But she seemed to have few interests and little fun in life. She was an art student. She worked a few hours a day cleaning instruments in Eastwood's laboratory. She was good, quiet company. This was why Eastwood, having no wife or family, had asked her to join the student Davis in watching for the new star from the high window in his lab.

"Do you really think it's worth while to wait any longer, professor?" asked Davis, trying to hide a yawn.

Eastwood was somewhat annoyed by the continued failure of the star to show itself. He hated to be called "professor" out of the classroom.

"I don't know," he answered sharply. "This is the twelfth night that I have waited for it. Of course, it would have been truly amazing if the astronomers should have solved such a problem exactly. They've been figuring on it for twenty-five years."

The new Science Building of Columbia University was a

towering structure of steel and cement. Eastwood's lab was on the next to top floor. Only the astonomers' rooms were above it. He had arranged a small telescope at the window. Below them spread the millions of lights of New York City, and far to the east, the dark depths of the Atlantic Ocean. All the streets were crowded, as they had been every night since the fifth of the month, when the great new star, or sun, was expected to come into view.

Some mistake had been made by the astronomers; though, as Eastwood said, they had been working on the problem for twenty-five years.

It was, in fact, nearly forty years since Professor Adolphe Bernier had first announced his theory of a limited universe at the International Congress of Science in Paris. Professor Bernier did not believe that the universe went on and on, outward and outward, forever. Somewhere, he argued, the universe must have a center, which is the point around which everything else revolves.

The moon revolves around the earth, the earth revolves around the sun, the sun revolves around some still larger star, and this whole system must surely revolve around some more distant point. But this sort of thing must definitely stop somewhere. The universe has to have a limit.

And somewhere there must be a central sun, a huge, fiery star which does not move at all. Because a sun is always larger and hotter than its satellites, the sun at the center of the universe must be of a size and temperature beyond anything known or imagined.

Some scientists said that this central sun, if it existed, should be large enough to be seen from the earth. Professor Bernier replied that some day it undoubtedly would be seen. Its light had simply not yet had time to reach the earth.

The passage of light from the nearest of the stars is a matter of three years, and there must be many stars so distant that their light has not yet reached us. The great central sun must be so far away that perhaps hundreds, perhaps thousands of years would go by before its light should burst upon the earth.

All this was just an idea at first. But about the year 2020, two mathematicians, Professor Morales of Princeton and Dr. Taneka of Tokyo, proved that Bernier's theory was right. It was shown that there really was an unseen sun of gigantic size, which, whether it was the central point of the universe or not, appeared to be without motion.

The weight and distance of this new sun could be figured almost exactly. Since scientists knew the speed of light, it was an easy matter to figure when its light would first reach the earth.

It was then estimated that the first approaching light would arrive at the earth in twenty-five years—and that had been twenty-five years ago. Now, three weeks had passed since the date when the new sun was expected, but it had not yet appeared.

Popular interest had risen and risen, excited by many newspaper and magazine articles. The streets were nightly crowded with people holding binoculars and star maps, while at every corner a telescope man had planted his instrument at a quarter a look.

Similar scenes were taking place in every large city on the globe.

It was generally supposed that the sun would look smaller than the moon, but larger than the planet Venus. No one knew exactly what effect it would have on the earth. Most scientists thought that since it was so far away, it would have little effect, and perhaps might be less bright than the moon. Still, some businessmen quietly rented large areas of the coast of Greenland, hoping that a great rise in temperature would force the world's people northward. The stock market went down, and a small religious group announced that the end of the world was at hand.

"I've had enough of this," said Davis, looking at his watch again. "By the way, isn't it getting warmer?"

It had been a cold February day, but the temperature was certainly rising. Water was dripping from the roofs, and from the icicles that hung from the window ledges, as if a warm wave had suddenly arrived.

"What's that light?" suddenly asked Alice Wardour, who was standing by the open window.

"It must be moonrise," said Eastwood, though the glow in the sky was almost like daybreak.

Davis forgot about leaving, and they watched the east grow pale till at last a brilliant circle of white light heaved itself into the sky.

It looked like the full moon, but much, much brighter. The streets grew almost as light as by day.

"Good heavens, that must be the new star, after all!" said Davis in a shocked voice.

"No, it's only the moon. This is the hour and minute of the moon's rising," answered Eastwood. He had just figured the whole thing out. "But the new sun must have appeared on the other side of the earth. Its light is reflected by the moon. That is what makes the moon so brilliant. The new sun will rise here just as the old sun does, but there's no telling how soon. It must be brighter than was expected— and maybe hotter," he added in a worried tone.

"Isn't it getting very warm in here?" said Davis, loosening his jacket. "Couldn't you turn off some of the heat?"

Eastwood turned it all off. In spite of the open window, the room was growing really uncomfortable. But the warmth appeared to come from outside. It was like a warm spring evening. The icicles were breaking loose from the building.

For half an hour they leaned from the window. They talked slowly and softly. Below them the streets were crowded with upturned faces. The brilliant moon rose higher. The temperature of the night inrcreased.

It was after midnight when Eastwood first noticed the reddish glow in the clouds low in the east. He pointed it out to the others.

"That must be it at last!" he exclaimed, with a thrill of excitement at what he was going to see, an event new to all humanity.

The brightness grew rapidly.

"Just look at it redden!" Davis marveled. "It's getting lighter than day—and hot! Whew!"

The whole eastern sky glowed with a brightening pink. Sparrows chirped from the roofs, and it looked as if the unknow star might at any moment lift above the Atlantic, but it delayed long.

The heavens continued to burn with different colors, turning at last to a fiery furnace glow.

Davis suddenly screamed. An American flag that had just been raised on a nearby tall building had all at once burst into flame.

Low in the east lay a long streak of fire which broadened as they squinted with watering eyes. It was as if the edge of the world had been heated to whiteness.

The brilliant moon faded in the glare of the new sun. There was a confused shout from the astronomers overhead, and a crash of something being broken. Then, as the strange new sunlight fell through the window, the three people leaped back as if a furnace door had been opened before them.

The glass cracked and fell inward. Something like the sun, but fifty times larger and hotter, was rising out of the sea. An iron instrument-table by the window began to smoke with the sharp smell of varnish.

"What the devil is this, Eastwood?" shouted Davis.

From the streets rose a sudden, enormous cry of fright and pain, the cry of a million throats at once, and the roar of a stampede followed. The pavements were choked with struggling, excited people in the fiery light, and above the noise rose the clanging rush of fire engines and trucks.

Smoke began to rise from several points below Central Park, and two or three church bells rang crazily.

The astronomers from overhead came running down the stairs, for the elevator had stopped.

"Here, we've got to get out of this," shouted Davis, moving toward the door. "This place'll be on fire soon."

"Hold on. You can't go down into that mob on the street," Eastwood cried, trying to stop him.

But Davis broke away and raced down the stairs. Eastwood got his back against the door in time to prevent Alice from following him.

"There's nothing in this building that will burn, Miss Wardour," he said as calmly as he could. "We'd better stay here for now. It would be sure death to get mixed up in that stampede below. Just listen to it."

The crowds on the street seemed to move back and forth like waves, filling the air with cries and screams. A cloud of dark smoke began to rise from the harbor, where a ship must have caught fire, and something exploded with a terrific sound. A few minutes later half a dozen fires broke out in the lower part of the city, rolling up mountains of smoke that faded to a thin mist in the dazzling light.

The great new sun was now completely in the air. The whole east seemed on fire. The stampede in the streets had grown quiet all at once. The people left alive had gone into the nearest houses. The pavements were black with motionless forms of men and women.

"I'll do whatever you say," said Alice, who was deadly pale, but strangely calm. Even at that moment Eastwood was struck by the beauty of her brilliant hair that burned like pale flame above her face. "But we can't stay here, can we?"

"No," replied Eastwood, trying to collect his thoughts. "We'd better go to the basement, I think."

In the basement were deep rooms used for the protection

of expensive scientific instruments. These rooms would provide shelter for at time at least. It occurred to him as he spoke that perhaps temporary safety was the best that any living thing on earth could hope for.

But he led the way down the staircase. They had gone down six or seven flights when a shadow seemed to grow upon the air, with a welcome relief.

It seemed almost cool, and the sky had clouded heavily, so that it looked like polished and heated silver.

A deep but distant roar started and grew from the southeast, and they stopped to look from a window.

An enormous black cloud seemed to fill the space between sea and sky, and it was sweeping toward the city. Its speed seemed to grow as they watched it.

"A storm cloud—and a tidal wave!" groaned Eastwood.

He might have known it would come, caused by the sudden heating of the air. The gigantic black wave drove toward them swaying and reeling. The winds came with it, and a wall of solid mist behind.

"Hurry! This building will collapse!" Eastwood shouted.

They rushed down more flights of stairs, and heard the crash with which the monster wave broke over the city. A rush of water, like the emptying of a huge lake, fell upon the street, and the water was steaming hot as it fell.

There was a tearing crash of falling walls, and in another instant the Science Building seemed to be twisted around by a powerful hand. The walls blew out, and the whole structure began to sink.

But the tough steel frame of the building refused to be wrecked. In fact, the upper part was simply bent down upon the lower stories, peeling off most of the shell of cement and bricks.

Eastwood was knocked out as he was thrown to the floor, but when he came to he was still on the staircase landing, which was tilted at a steep angle. A tangle of steel rods and beams hung a yard over his head, and a huge piece of steel had fallen straight down from above, smashing everything in its way.

The staircase was a wreck of plaster, bricks, and bent pieces of metal. Eastwood could look out in almost every direction through the twisted steel skeleton.

A yard away Alice was sitting up, wiping the mud and water from her face. She did not seem to be injured. Warm water was pouring through the cracks of the wreck though it did not appear to be raining.

A steady, powerful wind had followed the tidal wave, and it brought a little coolness with it. Eastwood asked Alice if she were hurt, without being able to feel any real interest in the matter. He wondered what had happened to his sympathy.

"I don't know. I thought—I thought that we were all dead!" the girl murmured, her eyes cloudly. "What was it? Is is all over?"

"I think it's only beginning," Eastwood answered in a dull voice.

The wind had brought up more clouds and the skies were thick, but shining white-hot. Presently the rain came down in almost boiling floods, and as it fell upon the hissing streets it steamed again into the air.

In three minutes all was choked with hot steam, and from the roar and splash the streets seemed to be running rivers.

The downpour seemed too heavy to continue, and after an hour it did stop, while the city remained in mist. Through the clouds of fog Eastwood caught sudden views of ruined buildings, huge heaps of junk, all that was left of the greatest city of the twenty-first century.

Then the rains fell again, like a waterfall, as if the waters of the earth were bouncing back and forth between sea and heaven. With a shaking of the ground a part of lower Manhattan went down into the Hudson River.

The strong wind drove the hot spray and steam through the shattered building till it seemed impossible that human lungs could get enough air to breathe, but the two lived.

After hours of this the rain stopped again, and as the clouds parted, Eastwood caught sight of a familiar object halfway up the heavens. It was the sun, the old sun, looking small and watery.

But the heat and brightness told that the enormous new sun still blazed behind the clouds. The rain seemed to have stopped and the hard, shining whiteness of the sky grew rapidly hotter.

The heat of the air was like an oven; the mists were blown away, the clouds licked up, and the earth seemed to dry itself almost immediately. The heat from the two suns beat down, down, down, down.

The twisted wreck of the building protected the two people from the direct heat of the new sun, now almost overhead, but not from the awful heat of the air. But the body will put up with almost anything, except being torn apart, for a time at least. It is the nerves that suffer most.

Alice lay face down among the bricks, gasping and moaning. The blood hammered in Eastwood's brain, and the strangest sights floated before his dreamy eyes.

His mind was not always clear. When it was clear, he decided that this could not last long, and he tried to remember how much heat would cause death.

Within an hour after the rain stopped he was painfully thirsty, and his skin felt as if it were peeling from his whole body.

This thirst and horror lasted until he forgot that he had ever known another life; but at last the west grew red, and the flaming sun went down. It left the familiar sun high in the heavens, and there was no darkness until the usual hour, though there was a slight lowering of the temperature.

But when night did come it brought life-giving coolness.

Although the heat was still bad, it seemed almost cold by comparison with the day. Most of all, the kindly darkness seemed to set a limit to the horrible events of the day.

"Oh! This is heavenly!" said Eastwood, drawing long breaths and feeling mind and body at peace.

"It won't last long," replied Alice, and her voice sounded calm through the darkness. "The heat will come again when the new sun rises in a few hours."

"We might find some better place in the meanwhile—a deep cellar; or we might get into the subway," Eastwood suggested.

"It would be no use. Don't you understand? I have been thinking it all out. After this, the new sun will always shine, and we could not live for even another day. The wave of heat is passing around the world as it revolves, and in a few hours the whole earth will be a burnt-up planet. Very likely we are the only people left alive in New York, or perhaps in America."

She seemed to have taken the lead with Eastwood. She spoke with knowledge, judgment, and calmness that amazed him.

"But there must be others," said Eastwood, after thinking for a moment. "Other people have found sheltered places, or miners, or men underground."

"They would have been drowned by the rain. At any rate, there will be none left alive by tomorrow night.

"Think of it," she went on, as if dreaming. "For a thousand years this wave of fire has been rushing toward us while life has been going on so happily in the world. No one imagined that the world was doomed all the time. And now this is the end of life."

"I don't know," Eastwood said slowly. "It may be the end of human life, but there must be some kinds of life that will go on—some germs or insects that can stand high temperatures. The seed of life will be left at any rate, and that is everything. Progress will begin over again, producing new types to suit the changed conditions. I only wish I could see what creatures will be here in a few thousand years.

"But I can't realize it at all—this thing!" he cried loudly, after a pause. "Is it real? Or have we all gone mad? It seems too much like a bad dream."

The rain crashed down again as he spoke, and the earth steamed, though not as badly as by day. For hours the waters roared and splashed against the earth in hot streams till the streets were foaming yellow rivers, dammed up by the wreck of fallen buildings.

There was a long rumble as earth and rock slid into the East River, and at last the Brooklyn Bridge went down with a crash and splash that made all Manhattan shake. A gigantic wave swept up the river from its fall.

The downpour stopped soon after the moon began to shine with brilliant light through the clouds.

Presently the east began to glow, and this time there could be no doubt as to what was coming.

Alice crept closer to the man as the gray light rose upon the watery air.

"Kiss me!" she whispered suddenly, throwing her arms around his neck. He could feel her trembling. "Say you love me; hold me in your arms. There is only an hour."

"Don't be afraid. Try to face it bravely," stammered Eastwood.

"I don't fear it—not death. But I have never lived. I have always been timid and confused and afraid—afraid to speak —and I've almost wished for suffering and misery or anything rather than to be stupid and dumb and dead, the way I've always been.

"I've never dared to tell anyone what I was, what I wanted. I've been afraid all my life, but I'm not afraid now. I have never lived; I have never been happy; and now we must die together!"

211

It seemed to Eastwood the cry of the dying world. He held her in his arms and kissed the wet, trembling, almost happy face that was strained to his.

The twilight was gone before they knew it. The sky was blue already, with streaks of red climbing higher and higher, and the heat was growing every minute.

"This is the end, Alice," said Eastwood, and his voice trembled.

She looked at him, her eyes shining with an unearthly softness, and turned her face to the east.

There, in crimson and orange, flamed the last dawn that human eyes would ever see.

Recall

1. The person who remains the least calm when the new sun appears is (a) Alice (b) Davis (c) Eastwood.
2. Eastwood suggests going to the basement because (a) of a special bomb shelter (b) the cafeteria is there (c) he thinks they would be safer there.
3. The Science Building is smashed and twisted by (a) an amazingly strong wind (b) an earthquake (c) a tidal wave.
4. At one point in the story, Eastwood and Alice have trouble breathing because the air is filled with (a) insects (b) hot spray and steam (c) dust.
5. On their last evening, Alice amazes Eastwood by calmly stating (a) a way to go on living (b) that she knew what would happen all along (c) the truth about their chances.

Infer

6. Eastwood is best described as (a) a colorful and funny man (b) a genius (c) a rather ordinary scientist.

7. One reason the scientific theory of Professor Bernier is described in detail is probably that (a) it helps make an unbelievable story seem more real (b) Professor Bernier was a friend of the author (c) the author considered the story only an excuse to present the theory.

8. Alice is "almost happy" at the end of the story because she (a) is looking forward to an exciting day (b) enjoys the suffering of others (c) has finally expressed her true feelings to another human being.

9. The main reason that the last sentence of the story is a very good one is that it (a) makes us see the scene as Alice and Eastwood saw it (b) contains more than one verb (c) really means the opposite of what it says.

10. When most people say "the end of the world" they probably mean the end of (a) human life on Earth (b) all life in the universe (c) all worlds and stars.

Vocabulary Review

1. Radio and TV signals that are sent by *satellite* are (a) harmful to radios and TV sets (b) bounced off an object in the sky (c) used for short distances only.

2. If a football team's offensive line is described as a *tidal wave,* the team is probably (a) weak (b) wet with perspiration (c) powerful.

3. A star that *glimmers* is (a) faint (b) bright (c) reddish.

4. People caught in a *stampede* are in danger of being (a) shot (b) drowned (c) stepped on.

5. If you have a *theory* about something, you have (a) a fear of it (b) total knowledge about it (c) an idea about it.

Critical Thinking

1. If you really think about it, you'll probably agree that "Finis" is one of the most impossible stories you've ever read. Yet somehow the author makes the events seem possible to the person who reads the story for the first time. Just how does the author do this? In what ways does he manage to make the story seem true enough to scare us?

2. Suppose that a second sun like the one in the story really did appear over a large American city. Do you think people like Eastwood, Davis, and Alice would behave as they did in the story? Do you think the crowds on the street would react in the same way? Explain fully.

3. In your opinion, who is the more interesting character, Eastwood or Alice? Why?

4. Because "Finis" is such a powerful story, it has been reprinted several times since it was first written. Once it was reprinted under the title "The Last Dawn." Where does this other title come from? Which title do you prefer? Why?

Acknowledgments

We thank the following authors and companies for their permission to use copyrighted material:

ACKERMAN AGENCY—for "Who's Cribbing" by Jack Lewis, copyright © 1952 by Better Publications Inc.; reprinted by permission of the author's agent, Forrest J. Ackerman, 2495 Glendower Ave., Hollywood, CA 90027.

ISAAC ASIMOV—for "The Fun They Had" by Isaac Asimov, copyright © 1951 by NEA Service, Inc., reprinted by permission of the author.

TIMOTHY D. BRUEY—for "Solution III" by Timothy D. Bruey. Adapted and published by permission of Timothy D. Bruey.

CURTIS BROWN, LTD.—for "Mr. Lupescu" by Anthony Boucher, copyright © 1945 by Anthony Boucher, 1969 by Phyllis White. Reprinted and adapted by permission of Curtis Brown, Ltd.:—for "Prolog" by John P. McKnight, copyright © 1951 by Fantasy House, Inc. Reprinted and adapted by permission of Curtis Brown, Ltd.

HYPERION PRESS, INC.—for "Finis" by Frank Lillie Pollack, edited by Sam Moskowitz, from *Science Fiction by Gaslight.* Copyright © 1968 by Sam Moskowitz. Adapted by permission of Hyperion Press, Inc.:—for "The Mansion of Forgetfulness" by Don Mark Lemon, edited by Sam Moskowitz, from *Science Fiction by Gaslight.* Copyright © 1968 by Sam Moskowitz. Adapted by permission of Hyperion Press, Inc.

VIRGINIA KIDD, with JAMES ALLEN—for "In Our Block" by R. A. Lafferty. Copyright © 1965 by Galaxy Publishing Corp.; reprinted by permission of the author and the author's agent, Virginia Kidd.

LOUIS R. LEIGH—for "Solution II" by Louis R. Leigh. Adapted and published by permission of Louis R. Leigh.

HAROLD MATSON CO., INC.—for "The One Who Waits" by Ray Bradbury, copyright © 1964 by Ray Bradbury, reprinted by permission of Harold Matson Co., Inc.;—for "The Gift" by Ray Bradbury, copyright © 1952 by Ray Bradbury, reprinted by permission of Harold Matson Co., Inc.

215